“Hey, I noticed that
weeds stuck in her mane.

Speaking without even looking at her now, he secured the saddle. “You know, if you don’t have time to groom your horse correctly, you don’t have time to own a horse.”

Her jaw went slack. She’d been riding her whole life. This was *her* horse and *her* barn, and this guy—whoever he was—had no right to admonish her. Questions swirled in her brain, and she spat out the first one she could latch on to. “Who on earth are *you?*”

Flashing a gleaming-white smile that dented a dimple in his cheek, he ambled toward her. He pushed up the brim of his well-worn tan Stetson, revealing tousled blond hair and a pair of eyes so clear and blue they conjured an instant image of Flathead Lake on a hot summer day.

She swallowed hard. As much as she hated to admit it, this guy was the best-looking thing to hit Thornton Springs since Jeffrey Mark Caulfield came to town to make that movie last year.

“Name’s Micah.” Stepping confidently close to her, he held out a hand. “I started work here this morning.”

Books by Lesley Ann McDaniel

Love Inspired Heartsong Presents

Lights, Cowboy, Action
Big Sky Bachelor

LESLEY ANN McDANIEL

Though she's a Montana girl at heart, Lesley Ann McDaniel now resides in the Seattle area. She juggles a career in theatrical costuming with writing women's and young-adult fiction, along with homeschooling her two daughters. In her spare time she chips away at her goal of reading every book ever written.

LESLEY ANN McDANIEL

Big Sky Bachelor

ISBN-13: 978-0-373-48679-3

BIG SKY BACHELOR

This edition published by arrangement with Love Inspired Books.

www.Harlequin.com

Printed in U.S.A.

But God forbid that I should boast except in the cross of our Lord Jesus Christ, by whom the world has been crucified to me, and I to the world.

—*Galatians* 6:14

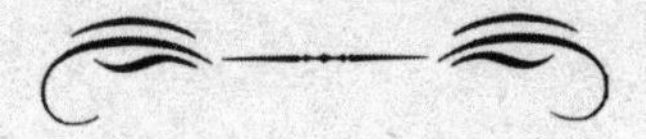

In loving memory of my dad, Leo Even, whose quiet support has been an ever-present blessing in my life.

Chapter 1

Janessa Greene could have sworn her old hatchback lost a little more oomph with each passing day. As she pulled off the highway and through the Bar-G Ranch gate, she sent up a prayer. No way could she spend money on her car right now—not with all the expenses she had coming up. Both she and her car would have to go the extra mile for just a little longer.

As she gunned down the long stretch toward the house, the sight of twenty or so impatient-looking parents standing outside their horse trailers made her stomach buckle. She checked the clock on the dash and grimaced. Why did they all have to be so prompt on the days when she was running behind?

She clattered to a halt between the house and the barn, then gathered up her work bag and purse. Leaping out of the car, she gave the parents a quick wave. "I'll only be a sec!"

A grating mixture of grumbles and moans followed her as she ran toward the front porch steps. She winced. Those folks had paid good money to have her teach their kids to ride this summer, and they had every right to expect her to deliver her best. She had tried to get there on time. If only the restaurant would stop being so busy on her class days.

She scurried inside, slowing only to push the door shut and to gather up the mail from the table next to it. Flipping through the stack as she bounded across the foyer, she held her breath. Today had to be the day.

"Argh!" She tossed the pile of pure disappointment onto the bench at the base of the staircase, gripped the bannister, and charged up. It was July already. Shouldn't she have heard from Le Cordon Bleu by now?

Reaching the top step in record time, she darted across the hall and into her room. She kicked the door closed, dropped her bags on the bed, and tore off her grease-splattered tee, then grabbed a plaid cotton Western shirt from the back of her desk chair. As she yanked it on, a rap on the door gave her a jolt.

"Ness, it's Courtney."

Her fingers found the shirt buttons as she searched the floor for a pair of jeans. "I'll be right out."

"I can go down and get the kids started if you want."

"Really?" Relief surged as she retrieved some decently clean Levi's off the window seat. "That would make you my favorite sister-in-law."

Courtney's laugh sounded through the door. "I'm your *only* sister-in-law. Besides, you know I love those kids."

Janessa breathed a little easier. The parents would feel better seeing Courtney, but she'd still have to hustle.

As she fumbled with her cuff button, her focus fixed on the poster over the desk. A plain chef's jacket hung on a fancy wire hanger with the words Le Cordon Bleu—*L'Art Culinaire* above, and the logo of the school below.

Leaving her second cuff undone, she tugged at the laces on her white SlipGrips—great for the kitchen but definitely not for the arena—and allowed her thoughts to stray. Le Cordon Bleu had been her dream ever since she'd realized she wanted to be a chef. Not only was it a great school, but they had a location in Seattle, not far from Thornton Springs. She bit her lip and yanked at the second lace. Okay, not too far to drive home for holidays and an occasional weekend, anyway. Montana only *seemed* like a million miles away from everything truly exciting in the world.

She kicked off the shoes. For as long as she could remember, all she'd wanted was to get out of Thornton Springs. Now that she had finally graduated from high school and worked for a year to save up money, her plans were just about to jell.

Flinging herself onto the bed, she quickly replaced her white Dockers with the jeans. She rolled onto her belly to reach under the bed, pulling out one boot, followed by a second.

She maneuvered into a sitting position, then yanked on the boots and scanned the immediate vicinity for her belt. Her eyes flicked across the framed photo that sat on her bedside table, momentarily sidetracking her with the familiar combination of comfort and sorrow that always accompanied it. Absentmindedly fingering the ever-present heart-shaped-diamond necklace at her throat, she wondered for the zillionth time how different her life would be if her dad was still here. He had her heart, even after he'd been gone for so many years.

Forcing her thoughts back to the task at hand, she plucked up her floral-shammed pillow from the head of the bed and let out a mini-cry of victory. She dove for a large gold buckle that peeked out from under her sloppily placed duvet, then swung her legs around and clambered to her feet. She quickly looped the belt into her jeans and grabbed a hair band off her bedside table, then dug through the pile of hats on the chair next to the door. She paused, running her hand over her Le Cordon Bleu ball cap. Her mind latched on to the one problem with her plan, the probability of which grew with each passing day: What if the school didn't accept her?

Shoving away the thought, she snapped up her favorite white cowgirl hat and plunked it onto her head. She just couldn't let herself think that way. It was only July. There was still plenty of time for her to hear from them. Besides, if she didn't get in, they'd send a rejection letter. No news didn't necessarily mean bad news.

She darted back out into the hallway and took the stairs two at a time, awkwardly yanking her hair into a ponytail as she flew.

Making her way across the drive, she saw that Courtney had gotten the class started preparing their horses. A few parents lingered along the outside of the fence, but most of them had left, probably furious at her for cutting short the hour they counted on to get things done while their kids were occupied.

Rushing into the barn, she grabbed a currycomb off its hook on the wall and greeted her horse. "Hey, Miss Molly." As she ran the comb quickly across Molly's back, she mumbled to herself. She'd have to do a better job of grooming her later on.

Tossing down the comb, she took up the brush. "Sorry, baby. You deserve better than this." Moving around to the horse's other side, she realized she'd left her second cuff undone. She fumbled with the button as she continued to brush Molly, but since she actually needed both hands to accomplish each task, she succeeded only in scratching her wrist with the bristles.

"Youch!" She jumped back, pulling up her sleeve to examine the scratch.

"Works better if you use the brush on the horse."

The confident baritone behind her nearly startled her out of her skin. She whipped around to see a guy hoisting a saddle up onto the rack on the wall, glancing over his shoulder and smirking like the feline friend of the recently departed canary.

"What in the..." Her tone came out a little more venomous than she'd intended, but he looked like a guy who could handle it. She'd been standing there talking to her horse. Why hadn't he made his presence known?

"Hey, I noticed that mare has some weeds stuck in her mane." Speaking without even looking at her now, he secured the saddle. "You know, if you don't have time to groom your horse correctly, you don't have time to own a horse."

Her jaw went slack. She'd been riding her whole life. This was *her* horse and *her* barn, and this guy—whoever he was—had no right to admonish her. Questions swirled in her brain, and she spat out the first one she could latch on to. "Who are *you?*"

Chuckling lightly as he finally turned to face her, he radiated an air of belonging that implied *she* was the outsider here, not him. His lack of a swift answer to her question gave the impression that he thought she should somehow already know who he was—like he was some kind of celebrity or something.

"Well?" She seethed. Not only had he made her even later by springing up behind her like that, but he had implied that she wasn't properly caring for her horse. And now he wouldn't even identify himself.

Flashing a gleaming white smile that dented a dimple in his cheek, he ambled toward her. He pushed up the brim of his well-worn tan Stetson, revealing tousled blond hair and a pair of eyes so clear and blue they conjured an instant image of Flathead Lake on a hot summer day.

She gulped. As much as she hated to admit it, this guy was the best looking thing to hit Thornton Springs since Jeffrey Mark Caulfield came to town to make that movie last year.

"Name's Micah." Stepping confidently close to her, he held out a hand. "I started work here this morning."

Oh. Of course. She'd forgotten all about the new ranch hand her brother, Adam, had hired.

Twisting her mouth in irritation at his obvious lack of first-day self-consciousness, she reached out for a quick shake. "I'm Janessa." Hoping to convey a lack of interest in further conversation, she returned to brushing Molly. Time was wasting.

"Pleasure to meet you, *Janessa*." After a long moment studying her the way he would an auction horse he was considering bidding on, he dipped the brim of his hat and strode out of the barn.

Her hand slowed on Molly's back as she furtively witnessed his exit. She gave herself a mental shake. What was the matter with her? Standing there gawking like a schoolgirl when she needed to get to her class.

Irritation swelled in her gut. Just what she didn't need, another pointless distraction from what really mattered—making the money to escape Thornton Springs and get her life off the ground.

As she hurried over to fetch her tack, her gaze again drifted to the doorway, but he had moved out of view.

Guys. That was one thing she just couldn't waste time thinking about right now.

She clicked her tongue. Of course, not thinking about them would be a whole lot easier if God didn't make some of them so all-fired nice to look at.

Micah thrust the tip of his shovel into the dirt, propped his foot on it, and leaned his arm on the handle. Angling back his hat and wiping his brow on his sleeve, he snuck a look at Janessa as she demonstrated cantering to a bunch of kids. Not only was that girl as pretty as a wild Montana daisy, but she rode a horse like an expert.

"...likely the biggest thing to happen around here in years." Owen, a ranch hand of probably about twenty, had spent the better part of an hour regaling Micah with the details of how Thornton Springs was "practically famous" because a movie had been filmed there the previous summer. "It's officially opening here this Friday. That's why there's so many tourists around town."

Micah grunted. He had only a passing interest in the topic. He remembered hearing about a movie being shot in Montana, but he'd been too busy with his own disaster of a life to pay it much heed.

"*And* that big movie director Travis Bloom bought the Circle-O Ranch right next to the Bar-G." Owen looked off in what Micah assumed to be the direction of said ranch, apparently highly impressed with his town's brush with the movie business. "The boss's wife works for him."

Appreciating the discourse, but only half listening to the content, Micah stole another glance at Janessa off in the distance. Her dark brown ponytail hung from beneath her cowgirl hat and bounced as she rode. She seemed so focused on the kids. He admired that focus.

It was plain as day she hadn't recognized him earlier in

the barn, but what had he expected? It wasn't like he had gone out of his way to tell Adam anything more than his ranch experience when he'd applied for the job. Not that he was hiding anything—he was just trying to find his way in the world now that everything had changed.

Still, it gnawed at him. He wasn't used to women acting the way she had around him, and that threw him like a mean bull. Would all women treat him that way if they didn't know who he was? Talk about a slam to the ego.

He muscled the shovel farther into the ground, then pitched more soft dirt onto the pile he had going.

Owen paused, apparently noticing Micah's distant focal point. "You met the boss's kid sister yet?"

"Oh, yeah." Allowing a slight smile, Micah nodded. "I've had the pleasure." He flung another shovelful of dirt as he watched Janessa give instructions to the kids. "That gal sure knows how to ride."

Owen leaned on his own shovel and ran his sleeve across his forehead. "That she does. Been riding since she could walk, to hear Adam brag about her. 'Course he's a mite biased."

Gripping the shovel again, Owen grunted. "Probably best to keep your eyes on your work if you favor keeping this job."

"Hey." Micah's defenses rankled. "I'm not thinking anything."

"Maybe not, but you should know the boss is extra protective of his sister. He's had to pick up the slack since their dad died about eleven years back."

Micah paused, allowing the shovel to hover in midair for a moment before plunging it into the ground again. Janessa had lost a parent. And at a young age, too. Could be that was why he'd felt an instant kinship with her.

He forced his focus to the ditch at his feet. "All I'm saying is she looks right at home on a horse."

"You should see her rope a calf." Owen sounded almost awestruck. "She's a regular champion of our little local rodeo."

The words hit a cold hollow place in Micah's gut. "No kidding?" His emotions ricocheted between admiration and anxiety, as a second wave of understanding washed over him. He'd found another area of kinship with her. In an attempt to conceal the impact of that groundswell, he kept the conversation safe. "So, this town has its own rodeo?"

"Oh, yeah. It's in August. Most everyone in town gets pretty worked up over it." Owen stuck his shovel into the ground. "You much into rodeos?"

Micah cast a fleeting look at Owen, gauging his awareness of the deeper implications of that question. His eyes returned to his work, assured that Owen wasn't guileful enough to harbor any hidden motives. He shrugged his response. "Not much."

"Me, either." Owen continued to dig. "I competed one time, but it didn't go so great."

"That's too bad."

"It's okay." Owen lifted a shoulder as though shaking off the thought and its attendant emotion. "I only did it to impress a girl."

The shameless admission amused Micah. "What was her name?"

"Her name's Keely. She's great. She's roped in our rodeo since we were kids. Trouble is she'll only talk to guys who are in the rodeo, so I pretty much don't stand a chance with her."

Micah kept silent. He knew that type, all right.

Continuing to work, Micah allowed himself the occasional glance at Janessa. She looked to be no more than twenty, with that innocent girl-next-door way about her. Not the type of girl he normally went for, but maybe that was because that wasn't the type who normally went after *him*. Her kind typically held back, looking all dreamy-eyed while the brazen ones charged to the front of the pack. Watching Janessa, he had to wonder if things might have been different for him in the romance department if he'd done more of the choosing and less of the getting chosen.

He forced his eyes off her and back onto the task at hand. It really didn't matter. It wasn't like he was looking for a woman to settle down with or anything. No way was that in the cards for him.

Suddenly aware of the hot sun drawing rivulets of sweat down his back, he stuck his shovel in the ground and moved toward the shady area next to the old garage by the barn. Tandy, the ranch cook, had left them a small cooler filled with water bottles. He grabbed one, cracked it open, and took a swig, then angled his head to peer through the window of the garage.

Adam had accommodated his request for a covered place to keep his truck, and Micah gave it a quick check. That and his bank account were pretty much all he had left of his old life.

Pleased to note that his truck had remained undisturbed, he shifted his focus to the old blue pickup next to it. It looked to be a Chevy from the 1940s. Quite a sharp contrast to his own rig, which was barely a year old and gleamed as new as the day he'd taken delivery of it.

"That's a nice old truck." He stepped closer, leaning in to get a better look. "Does it run?"

"Don't know." Owen had joined him by the cooler. "It's Janessa's, but nobody ever drives it."

Micah nodded. So the girl had an appreciation for old

farm trucks. Alarmed by his growing list of reasons to want to get to know her better, he determined to steer his mind in another direction.

He looked over at the house, which was at least ten times the size of the ranch house he'd lived in as a kid. This place *looked* like it belonged in a movie with its white siding and round towerlike things. That front porch alone was probably the size of their whole main floor back home.

Home. Funny that he should think of that word to describe the place he hadn't been back to in the twelve years since he and his dad had walked away. He choked down the hard knot that tried to creep up his throat whenever he pictured that place. That was so long ago, and so much had happened. But a part of him wanted to never forget what it had felt like to be there.

Not now, he told himself. *Let it go, Micah.*

Taking another draw of the cold liquid, he scanned the field where the lesson was still in full swing. "So, who are the kids?"

"They come from all over the county to learn to ride. Janessa's one of the best teachers around."

"No kidding." He looked up at her again, his admiration growing. So much for getting his mind off her.

"Yeah." Owen cuffed Micah's arm. "I hate to break it to ya, but she's planning on leaving in the fall for school."

Micah's heart sank a little, although that didn't make sense. It was good news that she'd be leaving. Great news, in fact. He wasn't about to get anything started with anybody, especially not the sister of his overly protective new boss. She'd only be a distraction, and that was one thing he did not need right now.

Forcing his attention back to the partially dug ditch,

Micah firmed his resolve. He wasn't about to let himself get roped in by anyone, no matter how cute she looked in or out of the saddle.

Chapter 2

Janessa peered through the oven window as though it had actual entertainment value. Who needed a big-screen TV when there was *choux* pastry to monitor?

Exhausted from her day of slicing and dicing at the restaurant followed by her spirited hour of teaching, Janessa's emotions were on edge. It didn't help that her mind kept drifting back to Micah. It had taken way too much concentration to try to ignore him watching her teach instead of focusing on the ditch he was supposed to be digging.

Oh, well. Knowing Adam, he wouldn't put up with that for long. He was probably lecturing the guy at this very moment about keeping his mind on his work.

Tandy looked over Janessa's shoulder. "They don't bake any faster by being watched."

"I know." She sighed. "They're not puffing up anyway."

As they stood side by side peering into the oven, Janessa's mood lifted just a little. She had spent so much time in the kitchen with Tandy over the years that she had come to think of her more as an aunt than the ranch cook.

The timer beeped, and Janessa reached up to turn off the oven. She grabbed a hot pad, then opened the door and pulled out the baking sheet, staring glumly at the perfectly browned, but perfectly flat little ovals. Discouragement rippled through her spirit. She had so wanted this to be the day she mastered the art of the cream puff.

"What am I doing wrong?" Her voice sounded like a cow stuck in barbed wire, but she couldn't help it. "I've been trying to get this down for so long. You've tried. Mama's tried. No one's been able to get to the bottom of why they keep flopping." She felt her lower lip protrude. This was a basic pastry. If she couldn't master this, how could she possibly think of becoming a chef?

"You'll get it, honey." Tandy moved across the kitchen, wiping her hands on the ever-present apron that covered her round form. "Just keep trying."

Janessa twisted her mouth and set the pan down on the big butcher-block table in the center of the kitchen. Maybe she could find something online after dinner that would help her solve this. A blog...a video...anything.

She huffed out a sigh. "I guess I can use them as lady-fingers in a trifle tomorrow night."

"That's the spirit. And tonight, you can rejoice in your victory over the potpie." Tandy pulled a large golden pastry out of the other oven.

"Pie's easy. It's as easy as..." Janessa considered. "Well, *pie*."

"Not for everyone." Tandy's tone turned thoughtful as she moved to check the stew she had simmering on the stove. "You should have seen your mama struggle with it at first."

"Seriously?"

Tandy nodded. "For months your daddy and I endured the tough, the soggy and the crumbly, not to mention the tears. I thought she was going to cry her eyes right out of their sockets when her first entry in the Thornton Springs fair didn't even win an honorable mention."

"No way." Janessa started to transfer the shells into a plastic container. "I thought she had always walked away with top honors in everything she entered. That's why all the ladies in town say she's the one to beat."

"That may be true today, but her first year all she walked away with was a complimentary dough scraper. It was downright humiliating to her."

"Wow. I had no idea."

"You know your mama doesn't like to brag, but that experience made her all the more determined to win a blue ribbon the next year." Her tone soothed as much as her kind face. "But remember, just because your mama has a reputation for winning all the blue ribbons in the county for baking doesn't mean that has to be your specialty, too. You make the best chili I've ever tasted, and that's a more practical skill than French pastries, if you ask most people around here."

"Thanks, Tandy." Lidding the container, she fought back her defensiveness. "But right now I'm not aiming to please the people around here. I'm aiming to please the people at my school. If they ever let me in, that is." She swallowed the sorrow brought on by that thought.

Even though she'd been accepted to a few other schools, her heart was set on Le Cordon. She had only applied to the others because people had warned her, in so many words, not to put all her eggs in one French *couffin* shopping basket.

She sighed. "Besides, no one says you can't be good

at all of it. Just because something's a challenge doesn't mean you ought to give up and just do what comes easy."

"That's very true. God gives us skills, but it's up to us to hone them. If you've got the desire to make a perfect pastry, then you just keep on working at it, and God will honor that." Tandy moved to pick up the pie.

"Let me." Janessa put on her favorite oven mitts—the ones with the cow faces that made it look like the cows were carrying the food in their mouths—and lifted the dish.

While examining how evenly the top had browned, she carefully followed Tandy into the dining room. She imagined she was about to present her creation to the jury at her exhibition at Le Cordon. Once in front of the table, she held it up proudly.

"Ta-da!" She looked over the top of the crust, expecting to see the supportive faces of Mama and Courtney, and maybe Adam if he'd made it in from the paddock. They were all there all right, plus someone else. Directly across the table from her, Micah stood with the corners of his mouth quirking. What was *he* doing here?

She froze, her pie hovering in front of her and her mouth hanging open.

"Oh, sweetheart." Mama clapped her hands together. "That looks and smells delicious." She gestured toward Micah. "Have you met our guest?"

All Janessa could do was give a dumb nod. Without his cowboy hat, his full head of thick sun-kissed hair just begged a girl to run her fingers through it. He was the kind of gorgeous that could easily rob her of all ability to speak and, judging from his self-confident cockeyed grin, he was well aware of it.

Snapping to alertness, she set the pie down on the table, a little too mindful of Micah's eyes zeroing in on her. She wanted to reach out with her cow mitt and wipe that self-satisfied smirk off his handsome face before he tried to point out her shortcomings as both a horse owner *and* a cook.

"Sorry I forgot to tell you we'd be having company, Ness." Standing at the head of the table, Adam pulled out the chair next to him for Courtney.

"There's always enough for one more." Setting down the salad, Tandy gave Janessa's arm an encouraging squeeze before going to finish getting the stew ready for the other ranch hands.

Janessa wanted more than anything to follow her to the safety of the kitchen, but she felt stuck in place. She looked over at Courtney, who made an exaggerated swipe across her own cheek, then flashed a look at Janessa's hands.

Her stomach jolted. No wonder Micah was smirking. She whipped off those juvenile mitts and tossed them onto the sidebar behind her, catching a glimpse of herself in the mirror as she did. *Ergh!* She looked like a disaster. Wiping the flour smudge off her cheek, she tried to send her mother a silent message to start dinner without her so she could dive into the kitchen to adjust her hair. Or better yet, disappear up to her room to starve rather than endure a meal with this annoying and yes, impossibly attractive guy.

"Sit down, honey." Mama was clearly oblivious to her plight. "We're all famished."

Facing the table, Janessa tried to collect her composure. So much for her mother's ability to read her mind.

Subtly smoothing her hair with the back of her hand, she slipped into the seat next to her mother. Adam pulled out his own chair and motioned to Micah, who gave Janessa a quick wink as he took the seat directly opposite her.

Trying to keep her eyes anywhere but on him, Janessa

looked to Courtney for support, getting a knowing look in return.

Great. Just what she needed. She shot Courtney a glare that she hoped communicated *Don't even go there,* but probably read more like *I know, right?*

Right. The guy was a hunk. So what?

She draped her napkin across her lap. Why was she letting him get to her? It wasn't like he actually mattered in the big scheme of things. There was just something disconcerting about the way he eyed her. Almost as if he knew things she hadn't given him permission to know. Maybe things she didn't even know herself.

"Dear." Mama reached out her hand to Adam, indicating that it was time to give the blessing on the food.

Oh, no. As Mama's other hand lingered just above the white linen tablecloth, waiting for Janessa to clasp it, she wanted to slink under the table and out of sight. With only the five of them at the long table, there was no one to serve as a buffer between her and Micah. If she waited till everyone else shut their eyes, could she get away with not taking his hand?

She made the mistake of looking at him as he observed everyone else joining hands. Taking hold of Courtney's fingers, he caught Janessa's eye with a look of pure challenge. Of course, she had no choice. Not reaching out would earn her a gentle reminder from Mama, which would only throw a spotlight on the whole awkward situation.

Micah arched one eyebrow, no doubt reading her thoughts with maddening accuracy.

Her hand felt like an anvil as she pulled it from her lap and thrust it across the table. Flashing a triumphant smile, he took it in his, then snuck another wink before shutting his eyes. Janessa rolled hers, thankful that all heads were bowed and her small gesture of rebellion had remained between her and the Lord.

"Father," Adam began. "We come together tonight, to praise You and to thank You for the blessings of the day."

Micah's hand felt reassuringly warm, reminding her of her daddy's work-roughened skin when he'd held her hand as a little girl. She pondered: how could Micah's skin feel soft and rough at the same time?

"Thank You for this delicious meal, Lord..."

Adam's strong voice prompted her to pay attention to his words. She was supposed to be giving thanks to their provider, not thinking about the hand that seemed to fit so nicely into hers.

"We give thanks also for our guest tonight. We ask that You would bless his time here with us at the ranch. In Jesus' holy name..."

"Amen." As Janessa's eyes slipped open, she met the amusement in Micah's incredible, and annoyingly deep, blue orbs. Glancing around, she realized that the collective attention of her family was focused on her hand, which was still joined with his at the center of the table. She let go so quickly, she practically tossed it at him. A blush crawled up her neck as she planted her hands in her lap. What a dope she could be sometimes.

"Where are you from, Micah?" Ever the gracious hostess, Mama smiled across the table as she cut into the pie.

He cleared his throat. "Up north, ma'am. A little ranch just outside of Havre."

"And does your family still live there?"

He shifted, as if something in her question made him uncomfortable. "No, ma'am. We sold the place a dozen years back." He held up his plate as Mama served the pie. "This does look tasty."

Janessa narrowed her eyes, sensing that his compliment

served more as a subject changer than a genuine courtesy. What was he trying to hide?

"I do hope you'll enjoy living out here on the Bar-G." Mama adopted her usual air of motherly concern. "There are other young men your age, so it's not as dull as it might seem."

"I could use a little 'dull,' truth be told." He set his plate down in front of him and reached for the salad.

"Well, it's anything but dull around here this summer." Courtney spoke as she passed her plate to Mama. "We're having a movie premiere in town next week."

"So I hear." He took a generous helping of the fresh greens before passing the bowl to Janessa.

"The movie was shot in Thornton Springs." Mama beamed with pride for their hometown's new claim to fame. "They even shot several scenes right here at the ranch."

Taking a stab at his salad, Micah looked up. "No kidding."

"Yes," Mama confirmed. "In fact, that's how we got to know Courtney. She came here to work on the movie."

Micah nodded in Courtney's direction, seeming to take a polite interest.

After giving a few details about how she had worked as the personal assistant to Angela Bijou, the star of the movie, Courtney continued her list of things to do in Thornton Springs. "…then there's the fair coming up in August."

"It's pretty small as fairs go." Mama sounded almost apologetic. "But folks around here get awfully caught up in the excitement."

Micah looked down, slicing his fork into the flaky crust on his plate. Janessa caught herself holding her breath.

"There's a rodeo, too," Courtney continued.

When Micah glanced up, his eyes flashed something. Fear? Concern? Annoyance?

Janessa narrowed her gaze, her curiosity piqued.

"Just a small rodeo," Adam added. "But the town gets pretty involved."

"I think most of our hands are competing in one event or another," Mama went on. "You could enter, too, if you're interested."

All heads turned to Micah, whose eyes grew round as two perfect sapphires. "I…don't have much interest… I guess." He moved a hunk of chicken around his plate, and looked over at Adam. "So, how many head of cattle you running?"

Janessa scoffed. Not only had he failed to comment since tasting the food, but he was acting like he had something against rodeos. Not that it mattered, but the guy was basically shooting down the two things in life, apart from Jesus and her family, that she loved the most.

Connecting again with those oh-so-blue eyes that she found dangerously fascinating, she swallowed hard. As far as she was concerned, this meal couldn't end soon enough.

After helping to clear the table, Janessa went outside and plunked herself down onto the porch swing. She gazed at the pink watercolor-washed sky and took in a restorative breath. This was her favorite time of day, when all the hard work was done and she could just relax and review her plans.

At the risk of falling dead asleep, she tipped back her head and allowed her lids to lower. She mentally calculated how much money she'd be bringing in this week, what with her classes, the overtime she'd committed to at the restaurant, and the catering gig she had with her best friend, Andra. If she was going to be able to swing the apartment move-in money, first semester tuition, all her books and supplies, and still have something left over to live on, she'd have to work like a plow horse right up until she left for Seattle.

She let out a little groan. With everything in her, she didn't want to have to take out student loans or borrow from Mama. She also didn't want to have to work while she was in school, but that would mean taking on overtime every week for the rest of the summer. Her boss would give her all the hours she could handle, but she had to know her own limits.

She quelled the quiver in her stomach that came only when she fretted over funds. Kicking the porch swing into motion, she tried to let her mind meander to something more restful.

Riding Miss Molly…petting her soft neck…weeds in her mane…*ergh.*

Okay, maybe not so restful.

Her mouth twisted. Micah had eaten two big servings of her chicken pie and had barely uttered a thank-you at the end of the meal. Plus, it seemed as though he had intentionally navigated the conversation away from the rodeo. Even if he wasn't interested, he could have just politely listened, and maybe even learned a thing or two.

Oh, brother. Good thing she was smart enough to steer clear of guys like him. Guys *period,* at least for the time being. She squeezed her eyes shut tighter. Surely God had a mind to use her in other ways. Maybe He wanted her to start some sort of program to teach restaurant skills to homeless people, or maybe—

"You know, you look mighty pretty when you're asleep."

Her eyes shot open. Micah stood in the doorway with his hat in his hand and that arrogant grin on his face, like he thought he owned the world. He sauntered out onto the porch, hooked a thumb in the front pocket of his jeans and leaned against the pillar in the manner of someone who intended to linger.

She sat up straight, suddenly wide awake. “Why do you keep doing that?”

His eyebrows arched. “Doing what?”

“Startling me.” His hawk-eyed focus on her rankled her tired nerves. “Like earlier, in the barn.”

“Sorry.” He grinned again. “Did you even notice the compliment?”

She crossed her arms, effectively blockading herself against his masculine appeal. He *had* called her pretty, which pleased some deep-down primitive part of her that she wanted to squash like a horsefly. He’d obviously mistaken her for one of those girls who had nothing better to do than swoon over any male who looked their way. That was *so* not her.

Flustered, her defenses kicked into high gear. “You aren’t here to give me another lecture on how to properly care for my horse, are you?”

His eyes tightened in apparent confusion, then widened with realization. “Oh, I get it now.”

“Get what?”

“Why you spent most of dinner firing bullets at me with your eyes. I didn’t mean anything by what I said.”

Firing bullets? Had she really been that obvious? She tuned down her defensiveness just a notch. “I know how to take care of my horse. I’ve been doing it since I was a kid.”

He held up a hand. “I just thought maybe I could help is all.” A corner of his mouth quirked as he regarded the porch swing with obvious amusement. “Do you always sleep out here, or do you actually have a room in the house?”

Maintaining her guard, she settled back a little into the cushion behind her. "I'm just tired from work."

"Understandable." His languid gaze lit on her. "Teaching looks tough."

"It is..." It grated on her that he seemed to assume teaching was all she had to do. "But I put in a full day even before that."

"Oh, yeah?" He slid into a sitting position on the porch rail. "Doing what?"

She hesitated. Was that genuine interest, or was he just making up for the horse comment? "I work up in Halston at Esther's Kitchen as a prep chef."

He crinkled his forehead. Well if that didn't make him even cuter. "So, you're a chef?"

"A *prep* chef. There's a difference." She paused, calculating how much she wanted to explain. "I help prepare the food. You know, chopping, grating. When we get really busy, I do some of the cooking and plating. To become an actual chef, I have to go to school, which is what I'm planning on doing in the fall."

"Huh." His eyes seemed to glaze over at that, and his attention veered to the purple-streaked horizon. "Nice night."

She shook her head. "You know, you're really good at that."

He looked her way again. "Good at what?"

"Changing the subject. Like at dinner." She slitted her gaze, interrogation-style. "When we were talking about the rodeo."

Drawing his brows together, he took a moment to compose his response. "I was just making conversation. *You want to talk about it now?*"

"It doesn't matter." She rubbed her upper arms to stave off either the oncoming evening chill or her irritation at letting herself be bothered by this. "I don't have time for the rodeo this year anyway."

"You're too busy earning money for school." It came out as a statement rather than a question.

"Right." She drew out the word, unsure of what to make of his insight.

"Too bad." He shrugged. "You'd make a mighty pretty rodeo princess."

A princess? Her mouth gaped open. What was *that* supposed to mean?

Before she could protest, he shifted gears again. "Tell me about that old truck that sits in the barn. 1949 Chevy Thriftmaster, unless I miss my guess."

She leaned back, still not sure if she felt affronted by the "princess" comment, but impressed at his automotive knowledge. "That's my truck. What about it?"

"I don't know. Does it run?"

"No. I wish it did."

"What's wrong with it?"

"I'm not really sure. It's just…you know…*old*."

"Where'd it come from?"

"It was my granddaddy's. I always loved it, so before he died he said he wanted me to have it."

"Nice. But I'll bet he didn't mean for you to be saddled with an old wreck just taking up space. You should get it running again."

"It's not an old wreck. It's a valuable antique." She folded her arms. "It's kind of silly to think of driving that old rig around Seattle." She smiled at the thought. "Sure would be cool though."

"Seattle, huh? That where you're going to school?"

She nodded.

Tapping his hat against his leg, he seemed to consider. "You ever live in a city before?"

"No." Her voice felt small. "I've lived on the ranch all my life."

"Mmm." He nodded sagely. "Well, be careful you don't wind up living in one of those big old houses with a bunch of people taking your food and skipping out on the rent."

Was he lecturing her again? "That won't happen." She pulled herself up straighter. "I already have a roommate and she's finding us an apartment."

"A roommate, huh? Someone you know?"

"Of course I know her. She's the daughter of an old friend of my mama's." She caught herself fisting her hands. Why was she feeling defensive again? "She lives in Seattle and she's excited to move out on her own."

"Oh." Even in this light, she could tell his eyes held a twinkle, like he was enjoying throwing her off balance. "Sounds like you know her *real well*."

She would have been thoroughly insulted if the comment hadn't been accompanied by a mind-bogglingly adorable smile. Her voice shrank in again. "I know her well enough."

With an *if-you-say-so* nod, he returned his gaze to the darkening skyline. "Seattle's a mighty fast-paced city. Be a big switch from living out here."

A slight pain gnarled her belly. "Everybody has to grow up sometime."

"I guess so. But does it bother you…leaving your family?"

The pain sharpened, making her regret that second helping of chocolate-pudding cake she'd had at dinner. No one, herself included, had dared ask her that question.

"I was more worried before my mom started seeing someone." Dipping her chin, she slid her diamond heart back and forth on its chain. "She's spending a lot of time with Travis Bloom." She gulped back a vague sense of melancholy. "You know, the movie director."

"Oh." His demeanor softened. "That must be strange. Because of your dad and all—"

"It's *fine*." Oooh. That came out sounding harsher than she'd intended. "I really like Mr. Bloom. Plus now that Adam has Courtney, I'm not worried about him."

"She seems like a nice gal." The subtle brashness returned to his delivery. "That's real good for guys like him."

Something about the way he said that nettled her. "What do you mean 'guys like him'?"

"You know. The settling-down type." He balanced his hat on his knee. "One thing's for sure, that's not me."

"Well…good." She bristled. Why did that comment get under her hide? "I…I mean, it's good that you're upfront about that so all the marriage-minded girls will know to stay away."

"Yep," he replied evenly. "All the gals know from the get-go what to expect. Nothing serious."

All the gals? Did he expect her to be impressed? She shook her head. "I think that's real sad."

"Yeah." A corner of his mouth lifted, on the side with that dimple. "That's probably because you're one of those 'marriage-minded' gals."

"I am not!"

"Yes, you are." He flashed a know-it-all grin. "I can tell by looking at you."

"You can't tell everything about a person just by looking at them. I'm not *ever* planning on getting married." The words pierced over the top of an exasperated breath. He was just needling her. Why was she letting it work? "Besides, if I did want to get married, I'd be sticking around here, not leaving for school."

"That might be true, but if tonight's dinner was any indication, you don't need any schooling. Seems to me you have all the cooking skills you need."

"You're kidding, right?" Her face heated. Did he think he was complimenting her? "I mean, it's not like I'm planning on majoring in Home Ec. I'm going to get my bachelor's degree in culinary arts so I can become a chef. Not so I can serve some man who doesn't even know a soufflé from a *chawanmushi*."

His brow furrowed over a look of mock injury. "Chaw… wan…what?"

At a loss for a biting comeback, she let out an ineffectual huff. "And let me tell you something else…" She abruptly stood, sending the swing into a frenzy of motion. "I'm a roper, not a *princess*." She whirled toward the door, fully intending to make a movie star–style exit.

"Not anymore." He spoke from behind her.

She reeled around clumsily, suddenly more Buster Keaton than Bette Davis. "What?"

"You said you're a roper. I just said 'not anymore.' You're moving on. Just like Owen."

"Like *Owen?*" That reference puzzled her. Owen had only competed in the rodeo one time, back when they were all kids.

"Right." He looked so sure of himself. "He gave up the rodeo and moved on."

Heat washed her cheeks. "So you're saying I'm giving up?"

"No. I'm saying you're moving on."

"What does it matter to you? You said you—how did you put it? Don't 'have much interest' in rodeos?"

He shrugged. "That doesn't mean I don't know all about them."

Taking a step forward, she symbolically recommitted

to the conversation. "Oh, you think you know *all* about them?"

"Could be."

Of all the conceited... She fumbled for a response. "I bet you wouldn't know the first thing about competitive roping."

A sanguine smile curved his lips. "I could take up tie-down roping if I had a mind to."

She glared at him. Was he serious? He thought he could just *take up* rodeo roping? He might as well try baking a batch of cream puffs while he was at it. "It's not the same as roping out on the range you know. It's a timed event. It's not as easy as it looks."

He regarded her with a wicked half smile and a glint in his eye. "You think I couldn't beat your time?"

"Are you kidding?" She advanced a step. "I've been roping all my life. I bet I could beat you without even trying."

"Okay." He dipped a nod. "You're on."

"What?"

"I accept your challenge. We can compete against each other in the rodeo and see who makes the best time."

"I wasn't really betting. And if you knew anything about rodeos, you'd know that men and women don't compete against each other."

A corner of his mouth lifted. "You sure about that?"

She hesitated. "Well…in team roping, it can be a man and a woman on a team, but—"

"Team roping." He seemed to consider. "Works for me."

"Are you even listening to me?" She flapped her arms. "You are the most self-absorbed—"

"Self-absorbed?" A crease settled across his brow. "What does *that* mean?"

She glared. "I just mean that if you want to impress people around here, you should try doing something for someone else instead of making yourself out to be some kind of—" she waved her hands in front of her "—big shot." She let out a breath, exhausted from this exchange. "I have to go to bed."

With a mini-hurricane of indignation raging through her limbs, she turned once more and headed for the front door.

"Night." He called from the porch in an unruffled, downright cheerful voice.

Banging the door shut behind her, she stood in the foyer, fuming without fully understanding why. Normally, she prided herself on having an even temper—a trait that came in handy in both the restaurant business and in working with kids. But right now her head felt scrambled. To make matters worse, Micah had remained completely calm, causing her to appear all the more irrational by comparison.

What was up with that guy, anyway? Not only was he full of himself, but he was hiding something, and she had to find out what it was.

The sound of Adam and Courtney laughing in the next room drew her attention. That was it. Adam had hired the guy. He had to know something about his past.

She cracked open the door to the parlor, where the couple sat watching the TV that was normally encased inside a retrofitted antique armoire.

"Hey. Adam." She spat out the words like watermelon seeds on a hot summer day.

Adam half pulled his attention from the screen. "Yeah?"

She slipped into the room, closing the door behind her like a spy. "Can I talk to you?"

Adam looked at Courtney, who gave a go-ahead nod and continued to watch the show. "Sure." He took his arm from around Courtney's shoulders and gave Janessa his full attention. "What's going on?"

She perched next to him, placing her hand on the back of the settee. "What do you know about Micah?"

He shared a glance with Courtney, who reached for the remote and hit Mute. "What do you mean?"

Brothers. She groaned out her annoyance at his inability to accurately read between the lines. "I think there's something he's not telling us about himself."

Adam ran a hand over his jaw, either annoyed or amused, or some combination of the two. "I know his name is Micah Brody and he has a lot of experience with horses and cattle."

"Micah Brody…" She frowned. Why did that name sound familiar?

He exchanged a knowing look with Courtney before reaching for the remote, a sure indicator that his involvement in this conversation was on the wane. "Why are you so interested, Ness?"

"It's not what you're thinking." A surge of defensiveness crowded out whatever remnant of mature thinking she had left. Her brother could reduce her to the spitting image of a four-year-old like no one else. "Something just doesn't add up. He seems like he's hiding something."

He rolled his head toward her, clearly ready to end the discussion. "He's not hiding anything, Ness. He can do the job and he came with great references. Why are you so curious?"

Good question. She shrugged. "No reason. Just concerned for the family business is all."

"Let me worry about that." He unmuted the TV. "You want to watch a movie with us?"

"No," she said distantly. "I have cream-puff research to do." She made her exit, annoyed that she had only made matters worse by giving Adam and Courtney the wrong idea about this. She wasn't *interested.* She was just… *Ugh.*

She made a beeline for the stairs, and didn't slow till she had reached her room.

Sitting down at her desk, she opened her computer. Her hands poised over the keyboard, prepared to type in *choux* pastry. Instead, when the address bar came up, she found herself spelling out *M-I-C-A-H B-R-O-D-Y.*

What was she doing? This was a pure waste of time. Still, she clicked on the magnifying glass icon and waited.

"'National Rodeo Champion'?" She clucked out a laugh.

Of course that was why the name was familiar. A guy named Micah Brody had broken a couple of bull-riding records and had recently won a championship title. But that couldn't be *him,* could it? She wavered.

Could it?

She clicked on the first entry and scanned the text. Sure, she loved the sport of rodeo, but she didn't follow it as rabidly as a lot of people. The very idea that she could have spent the past half hour talking…no…*arguing with* a national bull-riding champion and not even realize it….

She couldn't be that ignorant. Could she?

No. She refused to believe it. Micah the ranch hand couldn't possibly be *the* Micah Brody.

Determined to redeem herself, she scrolled down to a picture of a young guy on the back of a bucking bull, dust flying around him. The cowboy hat on his head cast a shadow across his face, so she couldn't quite make out his features.

"This is ridiculous." She clicked on Images and waited. She gasped. There were those magnetic blue eyes looking out at her. Mocking her. That was him all right.

She sat back, stunned. He must have thought she was a complete ignoramus. There she'd been going on about how she knew all about rodeoing, all the while proving that she was just an oblivious, unworldly small-town girl. She covered her face with her hands. How utterly mortifying.

Spreading her fingers, she looked at the screen again. Row after row of thumbnail shots of him hanging on to bulls as they bucked to a practically vertical position, or smiling confidently at the camera from underneath the very Stetson he'd been wearing earlier that day.

Accepting his national championship belt buckle. She leaned in to get a better look at that one. It just didn't make sense. What would a national rodeo champion be doing working as a ranch hand?

Humiliation met up with anger and sparked like wildfire down her spine. What kind of game had he been playing with her? Challenging her to compete against him in the rodeo without bothering to tell her that he was a professional bull rider? Did he think that was funny?

She was so mad, she could have spit bullets. What was she supposed to do about this?

And worse, how was she supposed to keep herself from hoping to catch a look at him again tomorrow?

Chapter 3

Micah hoisted a bag of feed into the back of his truck and tried, as he'd been trying all morning, to figure out where he'd gone wrong with Janessa the day before. She seemed like a great girl, but she obviously thought he was a first-class jerk.

Early that morning, she'd driven off in a car that looked and sounded like it could use either a tune-up or a trip to the salvage yard, and he figured she had gone to work for the day. Still, the notion that he might see her kept him from fully focusing on his chores. It had come as a relief when Adam had sent him and Owen into town to pick up a few supplies. Janessa had mentioned her job was in Halston, which he knew was a few miles up north. Going into Thornton Springs gave him a little break from hoping he'd see her.

A review of their first conversation only boggled his thinking more. He was used to being around people who valued his opinion about horses, but it was clear from her response to his helpful observation that she didn't know who he was. That was good in a way, since he'd been trying to escape the old Micah Brody and everything that went along with him. Deep down though, her reaction to him felt like a spur to his heart.

It hadn't gotten any better at dinner, or later out on the porch. If anything, he'd made it even worse. He had wanted to atone for the horse comment, but he'd been so nervous he hadn't known what to say. Instead of making small talk like a normal person, he'd resorted to his usual *big* talk. She must've thought he was making himself out to be some kind of Casanova or something. While it was true he'd dated more girls than he could probably remember, that wasn't exactly something he was proud of. Why had he even brought it up?

He shook off the thought, focusing instead on Owen's ongoing overview of the town, which was teeming with both tourists and locals.

"Over there you have the movie theater—they're getting ready to show *North to Montana,* the movie they made here last summer. Then there's the barbershop and the hardware store." A slight smile played on his lips. "Next to that's the ice-cream parlor. I never go in there on account of that's where Keely works. She's the manager now."

"Keely?" Micah frowned. "The girl from the rodeo?"

"Yeah." Owen nodded, his smile turning south.

"You mean to tell me you've been dodging her on purpose?"

"I just get so flustered when she's around." He lifted another bag. "I figure it's better to steer clear."

"Well, I'll tell you one thing for sure—you're never going to win her over with that tactic."

"It's not really a tactic. I'm just trying to avoid making an even bigger fool of myself."

"By hiding from her?" Micah chortled. "Interesting theory."

A couple of young women wearing jeans and lacy cowgirl shirts strolled down the sidewalk, slowing to admire Micah's truck. Then their eyes landed on him and they stopped cold.

He smiled inwardly. Now this was the kind of response he was used to. "Morning, ladies." He touched the brim of his hat.

Giggling at his acknowledgment of them, they continued on, casting flirtatious glances over their shoulders after they'd passed.

Owen rubbed his jaw. "See, a guy like you can have any woman he wants. Me…well, I'm a one-woman kind of guy. Keely's it for me, and I already blew it with her."

"You give up mighty easy, don't you think?"

Owen shrugged, as if he'd signed off on his fate and any hope of a reversal.

Micah shook his head. In a way, he envied Owen, thinking of himself as a one-woman kind of guy.

As they continued to load the truck, he thought about the way his own life had been for the past few years. Living on the road. The ever-present groupies—'buckle bunnies' as they were aptly named. It all added up to a pretty hollow life, one he missed only on a surface level, where his pride sat raw and exposed.

Those girls had always understood when he said he wasn't serious, and he'd just figured that was part of the game, kind of like a rodeo event. They knew they'd eventually get thrown off the bronco, but they all wanted to take the ride anyway.

None of them had mattered enough for him to even think about once he moved on to the next town. But Janessa was different. She was beautiful, with her long wavy hair and creamy skin that made her look like a china doll, but there was something else. Something he couldn't quite get a rope around.

That was why her remark about him being self-absorbed ate at him the way it did. It had come cloaked in a mantle of shame, serving as an unintentional reminder that his mother wouldn't be too pleased with the man he'd grown to be.

Maybe now was the time, in this new phase of his life, to reinvent himself. Stop showing off, and start thinking more about other people. He needed to prove that he could do something for someone else. A selfless act. But what?

After tossing the last bag, Owen nodded across the street. "You want to go over to Cal's Market to pick up some sodas for the drive back to the ranch?"

"Sure." That sounded like a fine idea to Micah, who was feeling the heat of the day even though it was only just past ten.

A minute later, as they entered the cheerful and surprisingly busy market, Owen greeted the man behind the counter. "Hey, Cal. Did you meet Micah yet? He's our new hand over at the Bar-G."

As Micah exchanged a greeting with Cal, he noticed a handwritten sign taped to the cash register that read Rodeo! Sign Up Here. His chest squeezed for reasons he couldn't quite tie down and wasn't sure he wanted to.

As he joined Owen at the cold-drinks case, the bell above the door pulled his eye to a blonde girl wearing a pink-and-white-striped dress, a little white hat and a very pretty smile.

Owen gulped and dove behind a laundry softener display.

Micah chuckled to himself as he contemplated the selection of sodas. It didn't take a genius to figure out who this girl was.

From across the store, she called out to Cal. "We're all out of chocolate syrup over at Moo, if you can believe it. With all these folks coming to town to see the movie, we're selling ice cream like it's about to be outlawed."

"I've been expectin' you to come in to sign up for the rodeo, Miss Keely." Cal spoke to her as he rang up the groceries for a young mom with a toddler in tow.

Keely's shoulders drooped as she filled her arms with bottles of syrup. "Not this year, Cal. I just never seem to be quite good enough to win."

"You can't give up, Miss Keely." Cal sounded concerned. "I thought you had a mind to join the professional rodeo circuit."

That caught Micah's attention. The girl was serious about rodeo.

"I think maybe it's time to admit I should stick to scooping ice cream." Her smile flatlined as she crossed to the counter and set down her load of bottles.

Glancing from Keely to what he could see of Owen, Micah had a moment of complete clarity. This was it. This was the thing he could do to prove to Janessa that he wasn't totally self-absorbed.

"Well," Cal continued. "I'm mighty sorry to hear that. You know, I haven't had one person sign up all mornin'." He held up a clipboard and flicked his fingers at it. "I think this might be about it for the competition this year."

"Actually..." Micah closed the gap between himself and the counter in two strides. "Owen and I are here to sign up."

Keely flashed a curious look at Micah while Owen made a strangled sound from behind the pyramid of plastic bottles.

Cal broke into a grin. "That's mighty good news, young man. We could use some fresh blood in our little rodeo."

He chuckled. "No pun intended, of course. What's your event?"

"Team roping." He looked in Owen's direction, hoping he'd catch a little of Micah's confidence and come out of hiding. "Owen on one team and me on the other."

"Team ropin', huh?" Cal shuffled through the papers on the clipboard. "Why, we haven't featured that event in more years than I can count." He found the right page and flipped the rest of the papers over the top of the clipboard. "Who will your teammates be?"

Micah tipped back his hat. This was going to take some finagling. He turned his gaze to Keely. "Well, I—"

Just then the door jangled again and a gaggle of teenage girls made a boisterous entrance. Micah tensed, on alert for what generally happened next for him in these situations.

The girls all chatted spiritedly, except for one—a pretty brunette whose focus immediately zeroed in on Micah. Her eyes expanded to the size of a couple of horseshoes as she jabbed the arm of the girl next to her.

"Look." The brunette's proclamation came out on a choked whisper.

The friend she'd jabbed looked at Micah, then yanked on the sleeve of the girl on her other side. "Tawny, *look*."

In spite of an apparent attempt at keeping their voices low, Micah heard them clear as anything. Judging from the heads now turning in his direction, so did everyone else in the store.

"Guys. Over there. Look." The first girl thrashed her hands wildly at her friends, ensuring she had all of their attention. "That's *Micah Brody*."

Her companions shrilled in unison, and Micah winced at the all too familiar sound. He braced himself for what he knew was coming.

The gang headed his way with all the subtlety of a stampede, their faces scrunched up in thinly veiled enthusiasm. He cautioned a glance at Keely, who now displayed the same wide-eyed excitement, having clearly made the connection for herself. Sometimes it took a while. Not everyone recognized his face, but most folks who paid any attention at all to the sport of rodeo knew him by reputation.

A burst of giggles followed as the girls clumped closer.

Well versed in the art of the meet and greet, he put on his best smile. "Well, hey, ladies."

The words were met with a round of blushes and renewed titters.

"Micah Brody. Sure enough. I thought you looked familiar." Cal stuck out his hand. "What brings you to our little town?"

This was hard to answer, since he wasn't entirely sure himself. "Well, I'm taking some time to enjoy working at the Bar-G. I wasn't planning on participating in the rodeo, but it seems I've gotten myself involved in a friendly competition with Miss Janessa Greene."

A noticeable reaction went up from the store patrons, who had slowly edged in closer.

"But…" The brunette worked her way in next to him. "I thought Janessa had decided not to compete."

"Well, it seems like she might be persuaded as long as we can get a couple of teams together." He nodded toward Owen, who now peered around the display. "We've got Owen to rope with her. Now all we need is another woman to be on my team. I figure we need someone with some experience."

"What about Miss Keely?" Cal flapped a hand, encouraging Keely to move forward.

Micah looked at Keely, whose eyes expanded even more than would have seemed humanly possible.

"Keely." He gestured toward her name tag, which was hot pink and shaped like a cow. "I take it that's you."

She nodded. "I…I've been roping since I was a kid, but I…couldn't…you're *Micah Brody*."

The girls spoke to her in low, animated encouragement.

Micah gave her the raised-brow look that had been known to sway the thinking of more than one young lady. "If I heard right, you want to compete on the national circuit?"

She nodded, her face becoming as pale as the white stripes in her ice-cream uniform.

"Tell you what. If you agree to compete on a team with me, I'll teach you everything I can about roping."

She opened her mouth but no sound came out, as if her lips had been frosted on her last foray into the ice-cream freezer. Seeming to give up on a verbal response, she resorted to a slow nod. The room broke out in a chorus of happy chatter, and the girls started to bob up and down as they surrounded Keely.

Owen had snuck around the other side of his barricade and now pulled Micah by the arm down the canned goods aisle.

"What are you doing? You know I can't compete in the rodeo."

"You're a ranch hand." Micah kept his voice low. "You know how to rope, right?"

"Sure, but I'm not any good at it." Owen's voice trembled. "When people are watching, I freeze up."

Micah gave his shoulder a reassuring slug. "Listen. If anyone can turn you into a first-class roper, it's me. You want to win Keely over?"

"Well, yeah…but—"

"Then it's a done deal."

Owen sputtered what looked like an objection, but came

out more like the sound people make when they have a dentist's drill in their mouth. Looking over Micah's shoulder, his face turned pasty. Micah twisted around as Keely approached them.

"Is it true, Owen? Are you really going to enter the rodeo again?"

"Why, sure it's true." Micah stood like a sentry in front of Owen, hoping his friend wouldn't bolt down the aisle and out of the store.

"This is a once-in-a-lifetime opportunity." Dipping her chin, she gave Micah the classic doe-eyed look. "I think I must be dreaming."

Micah smiled, pleased that, with Keely and her friends, he was back on familiar territory.

Now all he had to do was persuade the one person for whom his charm held no sway that she should go along with his plan, too.

After putting in a long day at the restaurant, Janessa walked into Joe's Diner with Andra, her best friend and favorite coworker. Spying an empty booth near the windows, they wound their way through the maze of mostly full tables.

Janessa continued to fill her friend in on the details of her exchanges with Micah. "It just seems like he's hiding something." Slipping into the booth, she took her phone out of her purse.

"Hiding something?" Andra set her laptop down on the Formica table and slid into the seat opposite her. "Like what?"

"I wish I knew. But every time anybody asks him about himself, he changes the subject real fast." Clicking on her phone, she checked for the millionth time that day for an update from her future roommate, Hana. She hadn't heard a word since Hana had started looking for apartments for them, and she was dying to hear how it was going.

Seeing that there were still no messages, she sighed and returned her focus to Andra. "It just doesn't add up. Why would he give up a lucrative career in the rodeo to work as a ranch hand?"

Andra shrugged, opening her laptop. "Something serious must have happened to him." As usual, she had her light auburn hair pulled up in a neat bun with a colorful rolled scarf wrapped from nape to forehead. Not only was she a sous chef extraordinaire, but she always managed somehow to look cover girl fresh no matter how many hours she'd put in or meals she'd cranked out.

"I have to get this figured out." Settling in, Janessa did a quick visual sweep of the room, wondering what had drawn this unusually brisk post-dinner rush. "Bull riders… Sheesh. I mean, any guy who wants to make a living by getting tossed around on a bull for eight seconds is just a different breed."

One corner of Andra's mouth lifted as she fired up her computer. "He's really getting to you, isn't he?"

"What do you mean?" Janessa unfurled the paper napkin which had been neatly rolled around her silverware.

"Oh, I don't know." Her voice held a teasing lilt. "You've been talking about him all day."

"I have not. Not *all* day." Janessa twisted the napkin in her lap. "I mean, you'd be upset too if some guy had totally tricked you." Glancing past Andra, she waved to a couple of women she knew, seeming to reinvigorate their already lively conversation. Puzzled, she continued her line of thought. "He could have at least told me who he is."

Andra started to type as she spoke. "You're not actually thinking of competing against him, are you?"

"No way. Besides, I think he was just pulling my leg. He's a bull rider, not a roper."

"Mmm..." Andra looked up from the screen. "I've seen some mighty handsome bull riders. Does he look more like Justin McBride or Sean Willingham?"

Janessa regarded her from under an arched brow. "More like a young Brad Pitt, but that's not the point."

"Brad Pitt." Splaying her hand on her throat, Andra let out a faux-dreamy sigh.

Janessa tossed her wadded napkin at her.

Batting away the paper projectile, Andra got back to business. "I know I said I didn't want to get too fancy with this food gig, but I have a couple of ideas I want to run by you."

Janessa bit her upper lip. She was excited about helping Andra with her booth for the movie premiere this coming Friday night, but it had become the straw threatening to break the camel's back of her already-packed schedule.

Andra went on. "In the spirit of our 'Hooray for Hollywood' theme..." She fanned out her hands at shoulder level. "How about chocolate-dipped star fruit?"

Janessa angled her a skeptical look. "I think that's a little *advanced* for Thornton Springs."

"You're probably right." Deflating a little, Andra gave her keyboard a few clicks. "It would be hard to get star fruit on short notice anyway." Her eyes ignited again. "How about baked brie made to look like reels of film?"

"I thought we were sticking with hot dogs and popcorn." Spotting Joe, the owner of the diner, wending his way through the room, she set her coffee cup right-side up. "When did this turn into *Vanity Fair*'s Oscar party?"

Andra sighed. "I know. It's just that if I'm going to set up my own catering business in this town, this is my opportunity to show what I can do. The exposure this job is going to give us is phenomenal."

Narrowing her eyes, Janessa leaned in. "Did you say *us?*"

"Us. Me. Whatever. My point is, there are going to be ten different food booths at this event. If we want to stand out, we have to add some personal flare."

Janessa tipped a nod of agreement. Ever since she could remember, Andra had dreamed of having her own catering business. Now that Janessa was habitually burning the candle at both ends, there were days at Esther's Kitchen when, if it hadn't been for her friend's ongoing chatter about her plans, Janessa might have just fallen asleep in the wild huckleberry buckle. She needed to be a little more supportive.

"Everyone's going to be impressed, Andra." She leaned on her forearms and gestured toward the laptop. "Show me what else you've got."

Returning her smile, Andra rotated the screen so they could both see it. She pointed at her research photos as she tossed out ideas.

Janessa's stomach tightened. This gig was just two days away. Between their full-time-plus jobs and Janessa's riding classes, how did Andra expect them to bake cookies in the shape of tiny Oscars, and red-carpet red velvet cupcakes draped with fondant filmstrips?

"Evenin', ladies." Wiping a hand on his apron, Joe filled both their cups with hot coffee to go with the warm greeting.

"Hi, Joe." Janessa grabbed the sugar dispenser and tipped it into the strong brew. She nodded toward the crowded room. "What's going on in here tonight?"

"This town's got rodeo fever. Worse'n I've ever seen it."

His look belied a weary but pleased reaction. "What can I get you ladies?"

"Apple pie à la mode, please." Janessa stirred her coffee.

Andra nodded. "Same for me."

"All right." Joe looked at Andra. "Tomorrow mornin' still good?"

Andra's eyes flitted to Janessa, then back to Joe. "I'm planning on it."

He smiled, then shifted his focus to Janessa and leaned in slightly. "And good goin', Janessa." With what would almost pass for a wink, he moved on to the next table.

"'Good going'?" Janessa frowned. "And what was that about 'tomorrow'?"

Exhaling, Andra moved the computer aside and rested her arms on the table. "You know how I've always talked about getting my own space for my catering business? I can't expect Esther to let me use her kitchen forever, and my cottage is way too small."

"Well…sure." Andra had talked about that practically ever since Janessa had known her, but always in a *someday* sort of way. Janessa hadn't considered that *someday* might come any time soon.

"I was in the Candy Castle yesterday picking up the Pixy Stix for our palm trees, and I overheard Cynthia and Skylar talking about how they hoped to have their kitchen moved in next to the candy store in time for the holidays."

"Next door? Not where the Mane Event is?"

"No way. Can you imagine this town without a beauty salon? They're moving into the place on the other side, where the used bookstore used to be. It's big enough for the candy ladies to put in a whole new state-of-the-art kitchen and packing facility that will open right into their store."

"Good for them. No more carting their chocolates down the street and around the corner."

"Right. Joe owns their old kitchen space and he needs to find a new tenant. The rent isn't exactly cheap, but I'm seriously considering it."

Swallowing a bitter lump of mixed feelings, Janessa nodded reassurance. "It sounds like it could be a good move."

Andra bit her lower lip. "I hate to ask, but do you have time to come check out the space with me tomorrow morning before work? It's a big decision and I really need your advice."

Janessa's dedication to her best friend wrapped around a knee-jerk refusal, taking it captive in her throat. She had promised herself she'd exercise Molly every morning, but how could she say no to Andra? She smiled sincerely. "Of course."

Andra broke into a relieved grin.

Joe returned and set two towering wedges of his famous apple pie, dripping with Moo's finest alluringly melty vanilla. He topped off their coffee and they grabbed their forks and dug in.

As Janessa closed her eyes to savor that first bite of apple-and-cinnamon perfection, the bell above the door sliced into her serenity. A group of girls she recognized as having been a year behind her in school made a lively entrance. One of them carried something that looked like a large roll of paper in her arms.

As a unit, they scanned the room, their collective gaze landing, surprisingly, on Janessa. She swallowed hard as the girls pointed and chattered to each other in undecipherable girl-speak.

That was the last straw for her tired nerves. "What on earth is going on?"

A couple of the girls took the roll of paper—or whatever it was—over to Joe at the counter, while Keely Rogers broke from the group and made her way toward Janessa.

Janessa drew in a breath. She only really spoke to Keely when she went into Moo for ice cream to go with a dessert she was making. Even then their only real topic of conversation, besides vanilla bean versus French, was the rodeo.

Keely's blond ponytail swung behind her as she trotted over to their table. "Oh, Janessa. Aren't you just so excited?"

Janessa exchanged a confused look with Andra.

Keely bounced on her toes like a show pony. "It's always been my dream to go into professional roping, but I know I've never been good enough. Now I feel like I might actually stand a chance. This is amazing!"

Half-formed questions fluttered around in Janessa's head as she waited for Keely to fill in the gaps.

"So I just wanted to say thank-you, because...well, I know this wouldn't be happening if it weren't for you." Breaking into the biggest grin Janessa had seen on her face since she'd gotten her braces removed two years ago, Keely swooped around and joined the other girls at a table they'd claimed on the far side of the room.

Janessa frowned at Andra. "Do things seem a little *Twilight Zone*-y in here tonight?"

Andra looked around. "If I didn't know better, I'd say people are talking about you."

"Me? But why—" Her phone began vibrating with the song "Brave" by Nichole Nordeman. A hasty glance at the caller ID told her it was Hana. She groaned. "Finally. Do you mind if I answer?"

Andra shrugged and returned her attention to the computer.

Scrutinizing the group of girls the way a lion would

eye a pack of hyenas, Janessa held her phone to her ear. "Hey, Hana."

"Oh, my gosh. You're not going to believe the place I found for us. It has everything. Two bedrooms with their own balconies, two bathrooms, a fireplace, a pool, free covered parking, a workout room. And there's a community room that you can book for parties. Way cool."

"Whoa. That sounds amazing, but how much does it cost?" She'd created her school year budget based on Hana's assurance that she shouldn't have to plan on more than three hundred fifty a month for her share of the rent.

"I'm getting to that. It's in an ultranice neighborhood. Pretty close to your school and to the boutique where—knock wood—I think I'm going to be working. It even has a name. It's called Cascadian Vista. Doesn't that sound way cool? We can tell our friends 'We live at the Cascadian Vista.'"

"Yeah, cool, but how much—"

"You're not going to believe it. It's only five hundred a month."

"You mean two hundred fifty apiece? For a two bedroom apartment?" She cast a look at Andra who returned a wide-eyed look of amazement. "That's unbelievable."

"There are deals in this city," Hana confidently crooned. "You just have to luck into them."

"Great. Let's go for it before someone else snaps it up."

"Hold on." Her voice sterned. "There are steps we have to take. I emailed the guy and he wrote back that I could drive by the building, which I did. It's even better than it sounds in the ad. It's all landscaped, and it's on a hill so we get a view of Puget Sound. If we get a corner unit, we might even be able to see Mount Rainier. When it isn't raining."

"A view? Awesome." Janessa was distracted by the sight

of Joe stepping up onto a small ladder behind the counter. Two of the girls held up the roll of paper, and he started to hang it above the board that proclaimed his daily specials. People had started to crowd around the counter, filling the air with an excited buzz.

Janessa frowned, trying to keep her attention focused on her conversation with Hana. "So, what's our next step?"

"Well, I emailed the guy *again,* and he wrote right back. I mean, like in an instant. He sent a form for us to fill out. I'm emailing your copy to you right now. Are you home?"

"No..." She watched as Joe pounded a few tacks or something into the wall, securing one end of the paper, then got down off the ladder as the girls supported the rest of the roll. "When do you get to see the apartment?"

"Just as soon as we get the form back to him. So I need you to fill it out, like ASAP. Where are you?"

"I'm..." She watched as patrons moved in closer and Joe shifted his ladder. "Shouldn't you get to see the place before we go to all the work of filling out forms? What if you wind up not liking it?"

"Janessa, we're going to love it. Don't worry. But I need you to go home so you can download this form and get it to me pronto. If we don't get it back to him, we could lose our place in line."

Janessa read silently as the girls unfurled what was clearly some sort of hand-painted banner. Thornton Springs Welcomes National Rodeo Star Micah Brody Vs. Local Champion Janessa Greene.

"What the—"

"I mean it. You snooze, you lose."

"Huh? Oh...I have to go." She clicked her phone off, glaring in disbelief. *"What on earth?"*

Andra looked up at the banner, which was garnering a considerable amount of enthusiasm from the other diners.

She clucked her tongue. "I thought you said this wasn't a real competition."

"It isn't." Janessa grabbed her purse and scooted out of the booth. "I have to go clear this up. Right now."

Andra frowned. "But what about—"

"Sorry, Andra." She tossed down some bills for her mostly uneaten pie. "We'll have to talk about the booth tomorrow. Right now I have a certain big-shot cowboy I need to set straight."

Chapter 4

Micah pushed his chair back from the table in the ranch hands' dining room, which was just off the kitchen of the main house. It felt good to eat home cooking, something he hadn't done on a regular basis in a very long time before coming to the Bar-G.

Even with his heavy workload all day at the ranch, he had kept his mind occupied, planning what to say to Janessa the next time he saw her. With any luck, he'd get to her before word got around that he'd gone and signed them both up for the rodeo.

He glanced across the table at Owen who, after asking all the obvious questions on the ride back to the ranch that morning, had been fairly silent all day. Micah was having a really hard time figuring him out. Couldn't the guy see what an incredible opportunity this was to win over the girl of his dreams?

Just then, Tandy reached around Micah to take his plate.

He grinned up at her. "I believe that was the best fried chicken I've ever eaten."

"Why, thank you." Her round cheeks turned pink as she added his plate to the stack in her arms, then scurried back to the kitchen with an extra bounce in her step.

"Don't get too used to being catered to." Hank, a jovial sort of guy in his midtwenties or so, elbowed Micah's arm. "Tandy cooks for us during the week, but weekends, we're on our own."

Leonard, the lead hand, chimed in. "Saturdays we take turns cooking over at the bunkhouse. We have a little tradition of breaking new guys in right away."

"Oh, yeah?" Micah gave a contented stretch.

"That means this coming Saturday you're up," Hank explained. "I hope you don't mind cooking."

"Not a problem." Micah pictured himself opening a can of pork and beans, sticking six spoons in it and setting it in the middle of the table.

"We expect a real meal," Jimmy, who looked barely out of high school, added. "You can't just boil hot dogs."

Liam clapped him on the back. "Jimmy tried that his first night and we almost boiled *him.*"

"It's got to be real food. That's the deal." Leonard seemed serious, like he was reciting the rules to a TV game show. "No boxes or mixes. Fresh vegetables. And it has to be edible."

"No scrambled eggs, either." Jimmy shook his head as if recollecting another ill-fated personal experience.

"And don't even think about ordering a pizza." Liam wagged a warning finger.

"No problem." Micah patted his belly. "I'll make you guys the best meal you've ever seen come out of that kitchen. There's nothing to cooking."

Something started to churn in his gut that felt suspiciously like panic. He had never cooked a meal in his life—had scarcely even boiled water. Now he was supposed to cook for a bunch of hungry ranch hands, and he couldn't just stick something in the microwave. What was with these guys? Did they harbor a personal vendetta against Birds Eye?

And why had he bragged about his cooking prowess, as if he actually had any?

As everyone started to take up other topics of conversation and rise from the table, Micah got the distinct feeling that Owen might be ready to break his silence. The two of them hung back as the others filed out the door to the yard.

As soon as it banged shut, Owen came to life. "It'll never work, you know."

"What won't?"

"Your plan. Janessa will never go for it."

"She will if I break it to her gently. You have to know how to handle women. Once I tell her about you and Keely—"

"Do you have to?" Owen paled. "That's kind of personal."

"She'll be on your side." Micah grabbed his hat from a hook by the door. "Besides, we'll need a woman's advice on this."

"Why?" Sounding a little panicky, Owen followed Micah outside. "*You* know all about women."

Micah smiled inwardly at the naive presumption. True, he had refined the use of an aptly timed word, a raised brow, or just the right hint of a smile to accomplish in seconds what might take other guys hours. But when it came to establishing an actual meaningful relationship, he was more in the dark than anybody. "I'm afraid I'm no expert at getting the kind of results you're hoping for."

Owen looked at him like a puppy who'd just been

scolded. "Right now I'd settle for not making her laugh at me again."

Hooking his thumbs in his belt loops, Micah started along the pathway that led toward the bunkhouse. "You have nothing to worry about."

It came as a surprise that he might have to prove himself to Owen. He wasn't used to people questioning his ability to follow through on his promises with absolute success. Failure, as his father had always insisted, was never an option. You keep going even if it kills you.

On the heels of that thought came the memories that Micah had done his best to bury for the past several weeks. He shoved them back down. No point in dredging all that up now.

Just as they stepped up onto the small front porch of the bunkhouse, the clatter of Janessa's car brought their attention to the driveway that ran up to the space between the main house and the barn. The vehicle lurched to a stop and Janessa leaped out, slammed the door, and charged toward the bunkhouse with a fire in her eyes that Micah could see even from that distance.

"Uh-oh," Owen muttered. "You're on your own for this one." He cracked open the front door and escaped inside.

"Hey!" Janessa shouted as she approached.

Micah moved to the edge of the porch, quickly recalculating his strategy. Obviously, he hadn't gotten to her in time.

"How is it that the whole town is under the impression that you and I are competing against each other in the rodeo?" By the time she'd finished the question, she had firmly planted her feet in the small yard of the bunkhouse and folded her arms in front of her, making herself look surprisingly fierce for such a tiny woman.

Assuming a casual stance that he hoped would encourage her to see reason, he let out a chuckle.

Her face puckered. "Do you think it's funny that I didn't recognize you?"

Seeing that the chuckle had sent the wrong message, he turned serious. "Now, just take it easy."

"Don't tell me what to do." Her fists shot to her hips. "Why didn't you let me know who you are?"

Since her volume had increased to a level that might garner unwanted attention, Micah started down the steps, his hands held up in a gesture of surrender. "You make it sound like I'm trying to hide something."

"Well, are you?" Her eyes burrowed into him like two perfect brown marbles.

His feet hit the base of the steps as he considered how best to answer that without either fueling her anger or telling a bold-faced lie.

The marbles slitted into two perfect almonds. "Well?"

He felt his reins on the conversation slipping from his grasp. "I thought it wouldn't matter to you." The second that was out of the chute, he wanted to herd it back in. He was supposed to be calming her down, not riling her up even more.

"*Wouldn't matter?* You tried to rope me into competing against you in the rodeo, and you thought it wouldn't matter to me that you've won championships all over the country?"

Micah grimaced. He'd liked it better the night before, when she'd seemed a little off her game. Now she appeared to be completely in control, and Micah, unfortunately, wasn't.

"Look, I'm sorry about that, but it's no big deal." *Oops.* What was it about this girl that made him blurt out all the phrases he knew he should avoid? Next he'd be saying something about her being too emotional or having a crisis. *Not good.*

"No big deal? Maybe not to you, but you can't expect someone to agree to compete against you not knowing—"

"So now you know. No big deal." *Really?* He might as well concede defeat. He was totally blowing it.

"You lied to me. You let me think you didn't even like rodeos. Then you said you could 'take up tie-down roping' like it was just that easy."

"Hey, I didn't lie. My event is bull riding. I haven't ever competed as a roper."

Her voice seemed to catch in her throat. "If you still think I'm going up against you—"

"I understand." He mentally clicked through his repertoire of past successful strategies. "You're used to calves, and you might not feel qualified to rope a steer."

"I live on a ranch." The glare she fired communicated that he'd picked the wrong strategy. "I rope steers all the time. That's not the point."

"Look." Moving closer, he patted the air in front of him with his hands, hoping to encourage her to calm down. "There's more to this that I have to explain to you."

"What more could there possibly be?" Refolding her arms, she lowered her voice a touch.

Aware that her willingness to listen might be extremely short-lived, he calculated his words. "Remember what you said last night about me being self-absorbed? That I should do something for somebody else?"

Those soft brown eyes creased, giving her a contemplative look that he found encouraging. "Yes…"

"Well, this is it."

"I'm not following." The line of her china-doll jaw hardened. "How is tricking me doing something for someone else?"

He cautioned a quick glance toward the bunkhouse. "Owen is crazy about Keely."

Her brows rose to a near knot. This was apparently news to her. "Okay. So?"

"So, Keely is only interested in guys who are in the rodeo. We need to get Owen into the rodeo."

Her mouth cut into a thin line of skepticism. "You think that Keely is going to be interested in Owen just because he enters the rodeo?"

"I think it's worth a shot." He maneuvered his head, trying to get her to make eye contact. "It's a good idea, right?"

She focused upward, pulling in a breath. With the release of that air, she met his gaze with seemingly reluctant surrender. "It's not a *bad* idea." The fire returned to her eyes. "But why do you need to involve me?"

A good question, and one that he wasn't quite prepared to respond to with complete accuracy. He would have to give her the answer that he could actually get a saddle on.

"Because it's not enough for Keely to just watch Owen compete. She needs to spend time with him. Get to know him. This is how I figure it." He held up a hand as if to paint the image against the evening sky. "Seeing as Keely and I are a team, we need to practice together. We need Owen and you there, too, so she doesn't get the wrong idea about being alone with me."

A laugh sputtered from her throat. "You think that just because a woman spends time alone with you, she's going to fall in love with you?"

"I just know how these things can go is all. I don't want her to get the wrong idea."

She shrugged her brows. "Go on."

"So I figure if the four of us practice together, that'll give them the opportunity to get acquainted. So I need you to be teamed up with Owen."

She regarded him in a slightly disapproving, slightly annoyed way that made his neck feel prickly. He had seen other guys get that same sort of look from girls, but being on the receiving end of it was new for him. He was used to the look the girls generally sent his way. That trusting, lash-batting look that said *You're perfect and you're my hero.* Janessa's look read something more along the lines of *I can see right through you, and I don't trust you one bit.* Much to his surprise, he found himself warming up to that challenge.

Her expression hardened. "I don't have time."

Choosing to see her objection as a request to help her justify giving in to him, he turned intentionally taunting. "Don't you want to help Owen?"

"Well sure, but—"

"Because believe it or not, romance isn't exactly my specialty."

She pursed her lips. "Yeah, I got that, Mr. 'Nothing Serious.'" Her eyes flashed with suspicion. "It doesn't have to be me. You could find someone else."

"I'm afraid it's too late for that. You're the local favorite. Didn't you see how excited everybody is to have us competing against each other?"

He'd taken a chance on that last line, judging from what he'd experienced from the grocery patrons that morning. Seeing her argument deflate, he figured he was right and she knew it.

She fired him a glare. "I'm just not doing it!" With that, she whirled around and stomped off toward the main house.

Micah drew in a long breath. Something told him convincing her was going to be harder than riding an ornery bull and even more dangerous. He smiled. Good thing he was well acquainted with danger.

* * *

The soothing aroma of chocolate hung in the air of the shop that had served as the candy store's packing facility for as long as Janessa could remember. Now, as she stood next to Andra, an unexpected lump formed in her throat.

"Well, ladies." Joe pushed some buttons on the wall by the door, bringing to life the old-fashioned fishbowl lights that dangled from the high ceiling. "What do you think?"

"I think it's amazing." Andra slowly took it all in, from the well-worn hardwood floor to the stamped metal ceiling. "It's bigger than I thought."

Joe fairly beamed. "The kitchen's a nice size, too. Let's go see if they might'a left any of their homemade marshmallows sittin' around."

Andra flashed Janessa a nervous smile as she followed Joe.

Janessa lagged behind, looking around the vaguely Victorian room. She traced her fingers across the smooth edge of a huge copper cauldron and lingered alongside the old-time taffy machine that she'd seen in motion a million times from the other side of the window. Although she'd never actually been inside this place before, she had treasured memories of it nevertheless.

She always made a habit of glancing through the large windows as she walked past, but her favorite memories were of her dad bringing her here at Christmastime. When she was small, he'd put her up on his shoulders so she could get a good view of the workers, dressed like elves at that time of year, making taffy and fudge, and packing hundreds of boxes with chocolates and other confections. She and Daddy would watch in fascination until they agreed that their toes were cold and it was time to walk around the corner to visit the actual candy store. There, they'd warm up with peppermint hot chocolate while making their official candy selections.

The memory warmed her, almost as much as that hot chocolate had.

Now as she slowly walked between the long tables stacked with rectangular white boxes, she thought about the delicious caramels, brittles, hand-dipped chocolates and other treats that had come from this place over the years. Who wouldn't be happy in here?

She made her way down a short hallway and into the brightly lit commercial kitchen, which stole her breath. Stainless-steel counters and vintage-looking industrial appliances lined three of the cream-colored walls. The other wall was mostly taken up by three tall, white-trimmed windows that looked out on the lot where Beau Healy kept the cars waiting for repair in his shop. Not very scenic, but it added a reassuring connection to the activity of the community.

In her mind, she could see a catering staff crowded around the large steel-topped table that ran down the center of the room, grabbing pots and pans from the racks above it as they busily prepared for an event.

Janessa felt instantly at home.

Joe was in the middle of supplying Andra with details. "Cynthia and Skylar are buyin' themselves a brand-new stove and refrigerator, so I offered to take these beauties off their hands." He patted the 1940's-era cast-iron cooktop as he consulted his watch. "Well, ladies. I'd best get back over to the diner before the breakfast crowd gets to missin' me too much. Take all the time you want."

With a reassuring bob of his graying head, he exited out the back door. The girls gave the kitchen another wide-eyed once-over.

"Well?" Janessa broke the contemplative silence. "What do you think?"

Andra slowly shook her head. "I think it's incredible. I see why Joe is asking such a high rent."

They headed back to the front room, taking in details like tourists in the Louvre.

Andra let out a resigned sigh. "I'm dreaming to think I could ever afford this place." She clutched her upper arms and slowly scanned the room.

Janessa swallowed her childish urge to yell *Take it anyway!* It would be wrong to influence her friend to make a decision she might later regret just to satisfy her own romantic notions of what this place might become.

"I had pictured something smaller." A sense of loss edged Andra's tone. "You know, a nice-sized kitchen with a cozy space at the front to meet with clients." She drew a half circle in front of her with her arm. "This is way more than we need."

Janessa cast her a sidelong glance. "Did you say *we?*"

"We. I. Whatever. It's too much space and too expensive."

"You're probably right." Janessa let her words drift out on a sigh, carrying a piece of her childhood right along with them. "It's a shame though, don't you think?"

Andra gave her a sad smile. "I've always loved this place. I'd hate to see Joe rent it to someone who doesn't really appreciate it." Andra looked wistful as they took a last lingering look around the room, then switched off the lights and headed into the bright outdoors.

"Want a lift to work?" Janessa had parked her car around the corner, surprised that tourists had already claimed the few spots along this side street.

"No, thanks." Andra hoisted her purse up onto her shoulder as they started toward the main street. "I can walk home and get my car. Besides, you have a riding class after work. You wouldn't have time to bring me back to town first."

"True. I'd have to corral you into helping out."

Andra tilted her a glance. "I'm afraid of horses, remember?"

"I remember." The words came out with a light chuckle. "What are you going to do when you fall for some cute cowboy?"

"Find me the cute cowboy and I'll work on my horse-o-phobia."

Janessa laughed. "Horse-o-phobia?" Her phone beeped, letting her know she'd just received a text. "The word is actually hippophobia." Still walking, she dug into her purse.

"No way," Andra said. "Then what do they call the fear of hippos?"

"I don't know." She flicked her phone on. "Common sense?"

"Very funny."

As they neared the corner, a couple of preteen boys rode past on bikes, whooping like they were on stallions instead of Stingrays, and distracting Janessa from the text she'd been about to read.

"Whoo... Hey, It's Janessa Greene!" One of them shouted as they looped back around.

"Can't wait to see you try to beat Micah Brody!" The other one swung his arm over his head like he was fixing to throw a rope. They continued up the block, hollering like cowboys and tossing imaginary lariats at everything from cars to pedestrians.

Janessa gritted her teeth. "See what Micah's done? Everybody in town is getting all worked up over something that's not even going to happen."

"You could stop by Cal's right now and take your name off that sign-up list."

Janessa clicked her tongue. "Micah's the one who signed me up. He can just unsign me."

They reached the corner and stopped cold, wowed by a gorgeous cherry-red Dodge Ram pickup parked two spaces in, next to Janessa's car. She let out a low whistle.

"You said it," Andra concurred. "Show me the cowboy who owns that rig, and I'll show you a cowboy worth curing my hippophobia for."

Jarring herself out of her stupor of automotive admiration, Janessa glanced down at the terse text on the phone in her hand. "Oh, no." She slapped her palm to her face.

Andra pulled her eyes from the truck. "What is it?"

"I can't believe I spaced out emailing that stupid form back to Hana." She shoved the phone into her purse. "It's all Micah's fault. If I hadn't gotten so sidetracked by that whole rodeo thing, I would have—"

"Uh… Ness…" Andra discreetly nodded past Janessa's shoulder.

Twisting around, Janessa saw Micah ambling toward them wearing a smirk that said she should pay more heed to her volume control.

She snapped back around, smacking headlong into her own inner conflict. This guy had done nothing but unsettle her since the moment she'd first laid eyes on him. But the feelings that stirred in her at the sight of him weren't entirely unpleasant.

This disquieting thought barely had time to take shape before its object sidled up to her with that slow, sure gait that made her wonder how many late-night John Wayne movies he'd watched as a kid.

He touched the brim of his hat. "Morning, ladies."

Ergh. She didn't have time for this. Not if she wanted

to stop by home on her way to work and take care of that form.

"You must be Micah." Andra flapped her arms up, then down, then up again like she didn't know if she wanted to shake his hand or take flight. "I'm Andra." She finally settled on offering to shake, then slid a perceptive back-and-forth look between him and Janessa. "Well," she said a little too brightly, "I need to get to work." With head bent toward Janessa, she added, "'Young Brad Pitt' is right."

Firing her a sharp arrow of annoyance, Janessa started digging in her purse for her keys. She stepped past the Dodge to where her car cowered in shame next to it. "I'm assuming you're in town to take my name off the rodeo sign-up."

"Actually..." He rubbed the back of his neck. "I drove in to talk to Keely about setting up a practice schedule."

"Oh." Where were those keys? And why did a twinge of fire shoot through her at the thought of him coming all the way into town just to talk to Keely?

"Besides," he went on. "I don't think I should take your name off that sign-up sheet."

Her eyes snapped up to meet his. "Why not?"

He raised and lowered a shoulder in a manner that emphasized the muscular shape underneath his deep green T-shirt. "Because I think you're going to change your mind."

She puffed out air, trying not to notice how white his teeth were. "What makes you so sure?"

"Because you love the sport of rodeo. And you recognize an opportunity when you see it."

"What kind of opportunity?" She fumed. How dare he presume to know what she was thinking? If there had been a shred of a possibility that she might change her mind, this was enough to kill it.

"The opportunity to learn from a pro. I can teach you everything I know about roping."

"You're a professional bull rider, not a roper." She burrowed down deeper for her keys. "You said so yourself."

"What I said was that I've never competed as a roper. That doesn't mean I haven't done my fair share." He paused. "I was fixing to compete next year for world all-around champion."

Her head jerked up again. Competing professionally in both events? *Impressive.*

She shook off the thought and returned to her search. There was nothing impressive about his arrogance. As far as she was concerned, any bull on earth should take great pleasure in bucking this cowboy right off his high horse.

Feeling a little ridiculous now, she took a break from the key excavation. "I've been roping my whole life. I don't need lessons."

"We'll see." He tipped his hat and stepped into the space between her hatchback and the Dodge.

She frowned. What did he think he was doing?

As he reached into the pocket of his jeans and pulled out a set of keys, it dawned on her. Of course a big rodeo champion would drive a flashy truck like this. She pondered. All the ranch hands she knew drove beat up old pickups, like her old Chevy…only newer. Why would a guy who could afford something like this need a ranch job, anyway?

The plot of this mystery kept thickening, just like a béarnaise sauce.

Chapter 5

"Nice truck," she called over the top of her car. "Why haven't I seen it at the ranch?"

Micah turned, looking pleased that she'd prolonged the conversation. "Adam's letting me park it in the garage out by the barn. I like to keep it protected from the elements."

Of course. But she didn't know whether it bothered her or pleased her that Adam had procured a roommate for Old Blue without her consent.

While Micah unlocked his truck and nodded a goodbye, she dumped out the contents of her purse onto the hood of her car. As his truck purred to life, an image shoved its way into her mind. Micah standing behind Keely, the sun glinting off her pretty blond hair as he held his hands over hers, showing her how to angle a perfect heeler throw.

Finally finding her keys, she tossed her things back into her purse, then got into her car. Of course, she had ridiculed his suggestion that it was a bad idea for him to be alone with Keely, but now she realized he might have been right.

That was silly. And why should it matter to her anyway? She thrust the key into the ignition and twisted. Instead of the uneven rumble she was used to, her engine clanked like a slamming prison gate, followed by a bonus grinding noise.

No! She checked the clock on her dash. It was almost eight-thirty. How was she going to make it home, fill out that form, and still get to work by nine if her car wouldn't start?

A bead of sweat broke out on her forehead as Micah's truck went silent. His door opened, and the next thing she knew he was at her passenger-side window gesturing for her to pop the hood.

Letting out a long breath, she complied. Her heart bucked like a bronco. She'd done lots of small automotive fixes. Why did he assume she needed him to rescue her?

By the time she made it to the front of her car, he had braced the hood open. Irritation instantly gave way to intrigue at the sight of Mr. Cowboy Mechanic leaning under the hood of her car, like he did this sort of thing every day.

She was struck speechless for a moment, until the irritation wheedled its way back in. "Are you sure you know what you're doing?"

Fortunately, he seemed to ignore the drop of acid in her tone. "I grew up on a ranch, too. It comes in real handy to be able to fix your own equipment."

"Well, I appreciate it, but I really don't need your help," she protested. "I'm fine."

"*You* might be fine, but your car sure isn't." He went to his truck and grabbed a rag from the back, then returned and pulled out her dipstick. "How old is this engine?"

"Ancient. Why?"

"It looks like it's leaking oil. You're going to need to replace it soon."

"The *engine?*" An image of all her hard-earned school money blowing away like leaves in the wind made her stomach turn.

He tossed her an offhand glance. "You on your way to work?"

Tension jitterbugged in her stomach. "I have to be there by nine."

Standing up straight, he dropped the hood shut, then wiped his hands on the rag. "Come on. I'll give you a lift."

Her hand shot up like a stop sign. "Oh, no. I—"

"What?" He tapped back the brim of his hat so she could get a real good look at those eyes that were even bluer in the morning light. "You got a better offer?"

Her jaw firmed. "I just need to have Beau take her over to his repair shop…" She waved a hand in the general direction of Beau's garage.

"You can do that later." His manner lost its sardonic edge. "I don't want you to be late for work."

As he moved around to the passenger side of his truck, a low growl burned in her throat. If he thought she was going to just jump into his pickup like one of his *gals,* he had another think coming.

Resting one hand on the top of the door, he raised a brow and a semi smile. "Time's wasting."

She looked at her watch. He was right. If she stood any chance of making it to work on time, she had to accept his help. With a resigned sigh, she grabbed her bags from her car and plodded around to where he waited.

She climbed in, noting the grocery bag at her feet. Apparently, meeting with Keely hadn't been the only errand he'd had in town.

He got in and started the engine. "You know, you really

should consider buying a new car before you take off across the country."

She gritted her teeth. Would it kill him to keep an opinion to himself? "Seattle isn't across the country. It's only two states away, and Idaho barely counts. Besides, I'm budgeted down to the dime. A new car will have to wait."

"It's up to you." He backed the truck out of its spot. "You can keep putting money into that old heap of yours, or you can decide to save up for something reliable." He gave her a sideways glance, then shifted and started them on their way. "You thirsty? I got a couple of root beers in there." He tipped his head toward the grocery bag by her feet.

"Thanks." She reached in, pulled out the sodas and noted the remaining items. "You planning on making something?"

"I have to cook dinner for the guys on Saturday."

"Oh?" She opened one of the bottles and handed it to him, then reached into the bag and plucked out a beet. "What's your plan for this?"

"Oh, I don't know. I thought I'd see where my creativity takes me."

She looked down at the other items. "You have macaroni, ketchup and rhubarb. You must have some really strong powers of creativity."

He leveled her a sidelong glance. "You don't think I can cook, do you?"

She shook her head and laughed. "No."

He slammed a playful hand against his chest as though he'd been shot.

Still tittering, she checked out the activity along the main street of town. Danita Parker stood in front of her salon, admiring a banner she'd apparently just positioned in the window which read Go Micah.

Something between a grunt and a hoot surged from Janessa's throat. This was her hometown. Why weren't people putting up banners for *her?*

"You know," she fired out, "for a guy who 'could use a little dull,' you've sure stirred up a lot of excitement around here."

"Hey, you're the one who challenged me, not the other way around."

"It wasn't a real challenge." Taking a sip of root beer, she shook her head.

"Well—" he raised a speculative brow "—what do you want if you win?"

Fine. If she was going to ride all the way to Halston with him, she might as well play along. "*If* there was a contest, I would want..." She pondered. What kind of prize would actually motivate her to enter into a competition? The answer came out before she even realized she'd thought of it. "This fancy truck of yours."

"My truck? Uh-uh." He sputtered out a laugh. "I'll tell you what, though. If you win, I'll let you *drive* my truck."

"Okay." Getting into the spirit of it now, she wagged a finger at him. "You'd let me drive your truck until I could afford to buy a new car. I figure you'd owe me that much."

"Oh, really?" He laced his tone with a playful wariness. "And what am I supposed to drive?"

She shrugged. "You could fix my car and drive it."

He considered. "Okay, fine. If you outscore me, we'll trade vehicles until you replace your car. But I get to have a look at your old truck and see if I can get it roadworthy. I'd rather be seen driving a vintage Chevy around town than something worthy of Fred Flintstone."

In spite of his insulting her car, a surge of emotion fired through her. She'd dreamed of having Old Blue running ever since she was a little girl. She used to pretend to drive it while Daddy worked on whatever car or tractor was parked next to it in the back garage.

She swallowed hard, rubbing her fingertips over the heart-shaped gem at her throat. "You think you could actually do that?"

"It's worth taking a look."

She studied him for a moment, letting the notion roll around in her head. When it settled, she was unclear whether she should take it as a bona fide offer.

"Okay, fair enough." Looking ahead, she folded her arms. "If I won, I'd get to drive your truck to Seattle, and you'd get to drive my fixed-up old Chevy. And if you won—" she eyed him sideways "—what would *you* want?"

Mischievousness glinted in his eyes. "If I win…" He held out the word just long enough to worry her. "If I win, you have to stay in Thornton Springs."

On a gust of breath she hadn't realized she was holding, she blurted out, "What?"

He held up a hand. "Let me finish. You have to stay in Thornton Springs until you can afford to replace your car."

She shook her head so firmly her neck cracked. "You can herd that idea right back into the chute, mister. I'm not putting off school for another whole year."

He shrugged. "That's the deal."

She huffed at his overconfidence. Did he actually believe she might agree to that? "No way."

"You don't sound very confident in your ability to win."

"I'm confident, Mr. Professional Rodeo Man. But you did saddle me with Owen. I hate to say it, but that's kind of a handicap."

"Have a little faith. With me training him, he'll be roping with the best of them in no time. And from what I hear…" He tossed her a raised-brow look she found alarmingly alluring. "*You're* one of the best around."

A blush wrapped her neck like a hand-knitted muffler.

"I don't know." She shook herself. What was she saying? "No. For the last time, I'm not going to be in the rodeo this year."

"All right." His confident tone implied a lack of belief. "Suit yourself."

She refolded her arms and looked straight ahead. What was it about this guy that made her feel as flimsy as an overcooked cannelloni?

Owen swung a lariat over his head and focused on the sawhorse Micah had fastened to the fence in the corral, angled so that its back legs sat a few inches off the ground. Drawing in a patient breath, Micah made a mental note to remind him that real cowboys didn't need to stick their tongues out in order to heel a steer.

The loop bounced off the top of the wooden frame and landed in the dirt a good two feet from its target.

Owen's shoulders drooped. "We might as well face it." Reeling the line back in, he shook his head woefully. "I can't even rope a sawhorse."

"Well no, not with *that* attitude." Micah moved next to him. "Do you want to impress Keely or don't you?"

Owen's chin dropped. "'Course I do."

"Then do the drill." He twirled his own rope over his head and tossed it, easily catching both hind legs in the loop. "It's a confidence builder." He walked over to reclaim his rope. "If you do it every day, you're bound to improve. Then you'll be ready to get on your horse and rope a real steer."

Looking unconvinced, Owen coiled his rope. "So, what kinda time are we shooting for, anyway?"

"The world record for team roping is 3.3 seconds. We'll be doing great if we get seven."

"Seven seconds." Owen gave a low whistle. "That's hardly any time at all."

"You're talking to a bull rider, my friend. Where I come from, *eight* seconds is an eternity."

Owen swung again, this time missing the sawhorse altogether.

Micah bit back the string of phrases his dad would have spewed out under similar circumstances. Instead, he uttered a more helpful, "You'll get it, buddy. Just keep trying."

In all honesty, Micah was starting to think he might not know how to help his friend overcome his lack of self-confidence. He could teach him the skills, but he had never seen anyone act so unsure of himself.

Giving it another try, Owen barely managed to land the loop under one of the wooden legs. "I don't know," he moaned.

"You've got to want it, my friend." He put his hand on Owen's shoulder. "Look, you're a ranch hand, right? What happens when you need to rope a calf out on the range for ear tagging?"

Owen halfheartedly coiled the rope again as he followed Micah to the cooler by the fence. "Leonard generally lets me do the tagging. I'm real good with the animals, but my roping skills aren't so great." He looked down, rubbing the back of his neck. "I think he's being nice to me on account of my rodeo incident."

Micah gave Owen a long look. "What happened to you anyway?"

Owen darted him a glance, then tossed his rope on the ground and leaned over the cooler, snagging two bottles of water. Micah accepted the one he extended as Owen went on. "Well, I was twelve years old when I first realized the only way to impress Keely was to be in the rodeo. I worked up my nerve, and entered the goat-tying competition." He took a long swig. "I figured I could ride Snowflake."

Micah cocked an eyebrow. "Snowflake?"

"The horse my sister and I shared," Owen explained. "My sister had taught her all kinds of tricks. I think what she'd really wanted was a dog."

Micah chuckled.

"I never paid much attention to what she was teaching her because I thought it was kind of, you know, *dumb.* All I knew was she used different sounds, like whistles and things like that, as her cues for these tricks."

Leaning against the fence, Micah took in a mouthful of water as Owen continued.

"The day of the competition, I was on Snowflake's back ready for my turn. I looked out into the crowd, and I saw Keely with all the other kids, waiting for me to go. She gave me a sweet smile, and I thought I had it made. My plan was going to work."

Micah nodded. "So, what happened?"

"Well, Snowflake ran out of the box just like we'd practiced, heading toward the goat. The crowd was cheering me on, and I felt like the king of the rodeo."

Micah knew that feeling all too well. That moment when the adoration of the crowd defines you. Justifies your very existence. But in a split second, fate can bring it all to a crashing halt. He was familiar with that feeling, too. He caught himself. That particular flood of memories was best kept dammed up.

"Then—" Owen's eyes got round "—something terrible and totally unexpected happened. We were almost to the center of the arena, when from somewhere up in the stands…someone…*whistled.*" His face grew dark at the memory.

Micah leaned in, riveted.

"Apparently, I should have given my sister more credit for her horse-training skills, because Snowflake stopped in her tracks and went down in this deep bow, which was the particular trick that the whistle was the signal for. You'd have thought I would've stopped, too, but no. I kept right on going." He moved his bottle to simulate himself flying through the air. "From then on, everything moved in slow motion."

Micah winced in empathy. He remembered that feeling, too.

"I flew right over Snowflake's head, with the goat looking at me like he wanted to say, *Hey, that's not the way we practiced it.* Then I saw Keely. Her hand went over her mouth and all I could hear was laughter. I'll never forget that sound." He paused, looking down. "The next thing I knew, I landed with a thud, sprawled out facedown in the dirt, and the whole crowd was laughing like they thought I was Jim Carrey. I swore I'd never compete in a rodeo again as long as I lived."

Micah put a sympathetic hand on Owen's shoulder. For a split second, he considered sharing his own story to let him know he understood. He stopped himself. What good would that do? It wasn't like he knew how to erase a painful memory. If he did, he probably wouldn't be here himself right now.

Instead, he gave Owen's shoulder a pat and uttered, "That's rough."

Owen shrugged. "I've learned to live with it." He regarded Micah through slitted eyes. "So, has Janessa actually agreed to this thing yet?"

Micah shrugged. "I think she's warming up to the idea."

"She's real good. I know *you're* a professional and all, but she deserves a shot at winning." Owen looked down, his eyes emanating pain. "I think maybe you should get one of the other guys to take my place. That would be more fair to Janessa."

"Owen." Micah jabbed a finger at him. "You're the reason we're doing this. Do you really want to see Jimmy or Liam riding off into the sunset with your girl?"

Owen kicked the dirt with the toe of his boot. "'Course not."

"All right." He bolstered up as much confidence as he could manage. "Then pick up that rope. You've got a date with a sawhorse."

Looking like a teenager who'd just been told to take out the trash, Owen retrieved his rope, shoved his empty bottle at Micah, and walked back to his throwing position.

Micah shook his head. What exactly had he gotten himself into?

Chapter 6

Janessa sat on the front steps of her house, eyes fixed out where their long drive met the highway. Since her car was at the repair shop, Andra had offered to give her a lift.

She gave in to a yawn.

Practically every minute of the past two days not spent working at the restaurant or teaching had been dedicated to helping Andra prepare the food and decor for tonight's movie premiere. Janessa had intentionally shoved all thoughts of the rodeo to the back burner, but now, as she sat looking out across the peaceful stretch of pasture and the deep blue mountains beyond, that particular pot started to simmer, then boil. Micah was trying to sidetrack her from her plans, and she couldn't let that happen.

No rodeo. That decision had been made months ago. She'd have to make sure he erased her name from the roster as soon as possible.

Taking a sip of strong coffee from her travel mug, she

reprimanded herself. After returning from her baking spree the night before, she'd stayed up way too late researching Micah Brody's rodeo career. She was paying the price in fatigue now, but at least she'd managed to find the answers to some, if not all, of her questions.

The melodious jingle of her phone gave a jump-start to her drowsy brain. As she pulled the device from her purse and saw Hana's name, a sickening realization punched her in the gut. It had been two days, and she still hadn't filled out that stupid form.

An apology tumbled from her lips even before she clicked Accept.

"Hana, I'm sorry. I—"

"No worries." Hana's crisp tone contradicted the reassuring phrase. "I didn't want to lose the apartment because of you not getting this one basic thing done, so I filled out the form for you."

"Oh." Uneasiness sidled up alongside Janessa's guilt over her inability to comply with a simple request. "What kind of information did it ask for?"

"No big. If I didn't know something, I just made it up."

Made it up? She wasn't thrilled about Hana lying on her behalf, but at least the ball was back in play. "So, have you heard from the guy?"

"Not yet. But the deposit cleared my account so—"

"Wait, the *what?*"

"Janessa." Her voice sounded stern. "You always have to pay a deposit when you rent an apartment."

"I know that, but...you sent him money?" Janessa's heartbeat quickened. "And he hasn't gotten back to you?"

"Don't freak out, Janessa. By the way, I drove by the complex again yesterday and I picked up a brochure from the office. This place is so amazing. They have a *movie room*. You can book it to host a private screening of any movie they own. That's cool, right?"

"Sure." Janessa calmed down a little. "That's really great."

"Luxury living. Plus there's this epic outdoor barbecue area where they have parties for the tenants in the summer. That's what the brochure says."

"It sounds nice. But..." She paused. "If you were in the office, why didn't you ask to see the apartment?"

There was silence, followed by a monotone "Why would I do that?"

"Uh...because you want to rent it and you haven't gotten to see it yet?"

"Janessa." The barely concealed impatience in Hana's voice reminded Janessa of a Sunday school teacher she'd once had. "I'm going through the proper channels. Did I tell you the place is cable ready and has free Wi-Fi?"

Even with Hana's reassurance, something still didn't sit right. "Okay. But don't you think it would be a good idea to look around at other places, just in case this one doesn't work out?"

"Doesn't work out?" Her words were like a cake of overconfidence topped with a prickly icing of irritation. "Just be patient. Oh, by the way, I found out this place has a gourmet kitchen."

Janessa frowned. Why didn't she lead with that?

"This is what the brochure says." There was a sound of paper rumpling in the background as Hana cleared her throat. "'Some elements that make this gourmet kitchen special are granite countertops, all new top-of-the-line stainless-steel appliances, a range with a warming drawer under the double oven, customized storage, a breakfast bar and a minifridge in the walk-in pantry.'"

Walk-in pantry? Janessa's concerns paled as she felt herself salivating under the influence of customized kitchen storage.

"It's all going to work out." The cheerful affability had returned to Hana's voice. "You can just send me the two hundred fifty as soon as you can."

"Wait…what two hundred fifty?"

"Your half of the deposit. It's not cheap living in the city."

Janessa sighed. She was learning that all right.

Putting away her phone, she looked across the mist rising from the lawn in front of the house and tried to picture herself on the balcony of her Seattle apartment gazing out over the pristine blue water of the Puget Sound. A bunch of cows became a pod of jumping whales. The distant bark of a dog turned into the cawing of a gull carried in on the soft morning breeze.

Closing her eyes, she imagined herself working on some school assignment and sipping a Venti Frappuccino from a lidded cup. She'd pause in her reading to look out over the railing and wave to a neighbor pulling out of her space in the lot below.

The toot of a horn yanked her eyes open. She realized that the sound of the daydream neighbor's car was actually Andra's old Creamsicle-colored Volkswagen driving up next to the house.

Scrambling to her feet, she shouldered her bag and trotted down the walkway. She greeted Andra as she climbed in. "Thanks again for the ride."

"It's the least I can do, since you're taking the day off work to do this with me."

Janessa fastened her seat belt and dismissed the unintended reminder of how much money she'd be making if she were going to Esther's today instead. She was always happy to help Andra and she'd been looking forward to this premiere for months, but now the pressure of her car and the apartment deposit made her wish she could just set up a money press out in the barn.

"By the way..." Andra sounded far too alert for a girl who'd been up past midnight airbrushing cake pops to look like kernels of popped corn. "Joe found a tenant. Some guy who wants to open a dental practice."

"In the old candy kitchen?" The irony made Janessa's teeth hurt.

Andra gave a slow nod as she pulled out onto the highway. "Such a shame." Keeping her eyes on the road, she shifted her expression from mournful to slightly impish. "Hey, did you get a chance to research your rodeo man?"

"He's not *my* anything." Janessa rolled her eyes. "But yes, I went online and dug a little deeper. Apparently his dad worked for a stock contractor, so Micah traveled with him on the rodeo circuit. He started competing when he was ten."

"Wow. What a life."

"I'll say. Anyway, he won a bunch of junior championships and became a professional bull rider when he turned eighteen. Lots of people had him pegged to win the nationals this year, but he got injured and didn't go back. That's where his story pretty much stops."

By the time Janessa had filled in all the details, they were pulling into the fairgrounds. Andra parked and they both grabbed their bags and got out of the car.

"So..." Janessa met Andra at the front of the Volkswagen. "I can understand him not wanting to go back to the rodeo, or maybe not being able to, but it still doesn't explain why he took a job as a ranch hand. According to what I saw online, he won plenty of money over the last few years." She shoved Andra's catering banner under one arm, and the large menu board they'd carefully hand painted under the other.

"Maybe he likes ranch work." Having taken up a box of supplies, Andra slammed the trunk shut.

"Maybe. But why not buy his own?" Janessa struggled to get a good grip on the board as they started toward the rodeo buildings. "The guys who make it to that level are the ones who buy those huge spreads and get streets named after them in their hometowns."

Being careful not to step on the long red tarp that a couple of guys from the hardware store were spreading out to simulate a red carpet, they slid through double doors and into the auction building.

After tonight, the movie would be shown at the theater in town, but with so many people expected for the premiere, the town council had figured the only place big enough was the livestock pavilion. It might be a little rustic, but it already had some seating, and the high-up windows could easily be covered to shut out the light.

Stopping to get their bearings, they scanned the huge hall.

A crew of guys in cowboy hats were setting up chairs in the area where the livestock was paraded on auction days. Another bunch was cleaning off the wall that the movie would be projected onto. If it hadn't been for the lingering aroma of hay and horses, the place might almost have been mistaken for a Hollywood movie palace.

"Come on." Andra gestured with her shoulder to the loftlike upper level, where several built-in concession stands looked down over the pavilion. "Our booth is right at the top of the stairs. Prime real estate."

Following Andra up the long wooden staircase, Janessa noticed something strange. Several of the women and girls who were helping hang twinkle lights and set up booths wore silver-dollar-sized bright yellow buttons with red lettering on their shirts.

Flattening herself and her signs against the railing so a woman carrying a coil of red velvet rope could pass, Janessa got a good look at her button. She nearly dropped the menu board. "'The Micah Brody Fan Club'?" Regaining her grip, she hurried up the last of the steps.

"Excuse me." She stooped to address a teenage girl who was placing large gold-painted cardboard stars along the exhibition walkway to simulate the Hollywood Walk of Fame. "Where is everybody getting those buttons?"

The girl pointed to where a crowd had gathered on the other side of the U-shaped loft. "Over there at the Mane Event stand. Danita is giving out shampoo samples and signing people up for the club."

Janessa muttered as she sidestepped over to where Andra stood surveying their area. "That's just unbelievable." She eased the menu board onto the floor, leaning it against the front of the booth. "I know he's a big celebrity and everything, but I've ridden in this rodeo my whole life. Isn't anybody going to start a fan club for me?"

"I'll be your fan club." Andra laughed as she helped Janessa lift the banner onto the front counter. "I bet I can get your mama to join, too." She pulled a movie clapper board that Courtney had borrowed for them out of her box, and set it on top of the glass pastry case. "Let's get started."

"If you ask me..." Janessa unpacked the flowerpot they'd painted to look like a huge popcorn tub. "A fan club is nothing more than idol worship. Rodeo is just a sport, after all. It's not like it's going to change the world."

"Hey, if I didn't know better," a male voice piped up from behind her, "I'd say you had something against rodeos."

She whirled around, nearly dropping the flowerpot.

Micah stood there holding a Hollywood and Vine street sign that someone had made out of old boards and some fence pipe. Heat washed her cheeks. How did he manage to always appear at the worst possible moments?

She cleared her throat in a feeble attempt to compose herself. "What are you doing here?"

"Didn't Adam tell you?" He walked the sign over to the railing that edged the loft and set it down. "He sent us here this morning to help. Apparently there's a lot *to* putting on a highfalutin movie premiere."

She turned away, pretending to ignore her rush of self-consciousness over the fact that she'd researched this guy like a journalist—or an obsessed fan—the night before.

All the articles she'd read flashed through her mind as she sensed him moving closer. Much to her amazement, the exasperation that had been her prevailing emotion all week had been reduced to a sweet syrup of admiration. Micah had worked hard his whole life to become one of the top competitors in the most dangerous sport in the world. How could she not admire that?

Plus, the thought of his being severely injured while competing made her feel strangely protective of him.

She attempted to get a grip. What small-town girl's head wouldn't turn at the sight of a rugged cowboy, after all? It was just because she'd lived in this one-horse town her whole life, where cowboys were as common as wildflowers. By the time she'd spent a semester in Seattle, they would lose their appeal. She was certain of it.

Trying her best to just ignore him, she continued to unpack. All she needed to do was get out of Dodge, and her head would be cleared of him.

"Morning, all."

Janessa looked up to see Hank wheeling a hand truck loaded with boxes into their booth.

"Here's the popcorn you ordered from Cal. You sure do plan on selling a lot of it."

"It is a movie, after all." A slight rosiness tinted Andra's cheeks. "Can you still drive me over to Esther's to pick up our baked goods?"

Hank unloaded the boxes. "I got my truck parked out back."

"Great." Andra looked at Janessa. "Do you mind starting the decorating while I'm gone?"

"No problem." Janessa took the paper palm leaves out of a box and started attaching them to the tops of the Pixy Stix tree trunks.

As Andra left with Hank, Micah tipped his hat back and put his hands on his hips. "Looks like that leaves me to be your handyman. What do you need done?"

She looked over at him as he flashed that dimple, and her mind went blank. *Need done? What?*

Making no effort to conceal his amusement, he quirked a brow. "Why don't I just grab a ladder, and I can put up your signs." He dipped his chin in the direction of the menu board.

Aware that he had used the chin gesture as an impetus to inch closer, Janessa gulped. Her hand froze on a paper palm frond.

"I...need...*signs*..." The ability to form complete sentences was apparently lodged in the part of her brain that had shut down for maintenance the moment he'd drawn nearer.

One corner of his mouth lifted slightly and he took a couple of slow steps backward, his eyes still riveted to hers. Finally, he broke the gaze and turned to go.

Breathable air seemed suddenly to be at a premium as she watched him amble to the end of the loft, where some guys were hanging a couple of bigger-than-life-size posters of Angela Bijou and Jeffrey Mark Caulfield.

Her knees wobbling like jelly, she braced herself on the counter. She might as well face it.

She'd officially become a Micah Brody fan.

By the time Micah returned with the ladder, Janessa was standing inside the booth, madly gluing little wads of white paper to the top of a big popcorn tub and acting like she didn't see him.

Keeping his enjoyment of her little acting job to himself, he picked up a menu board and eyed the back wall of the booth. "You want this up there?"

Finally looking up, she nodded and stepped to one side to accommodate the ladder in the small space. Looking a little ill at ease, she returned to her gluing. "You figure out what you're cooking for the guys tomorrow night?"

The question delivered up a combo plate of feelings. Annoyance at the reminder of the meal he had yet to plan, and pleasure at her concern over it.

He examined the row of screw heads protruding from the wall, clearly meant for hanging signage. "It'll come together as it comes together."

"In other words..." Her tone came out lined with a sharp edge of snideness. "You have no idea."

He fought back a grimace. It was bad enough he was going to fail miserably in front of the guys. He really didn't want to have to admit his shortcomings to Janessa.

He eased the board onto the screw heads. "You get a diagnosis on your car yet?"

As she opened up the big glass case next to the cash register, she puffed out air. "You shouldn't always do that."

"What?" Placing his fingers on the top rim of the sign, he gave it a push to test its stability.

"Change the subject." She placed the paper popcorn tub inside the glass case. "It makes you hard to follow."

He started down the ladder. "Some women see that as a challenge."

Her mouth twisted, and he knew exactly what she was thinking. Why did the compulsion to remind her that he was a magnet to females seem to drive their every conversation?

As he folded up the ladder, he wanted to tell her that it was his celebrity status, not him, that was the magnet. That he'd enjoyed it at first, but deep down he had always resented it. And that one of the things he liked most about her was that she wasn't like all the other girls.

Instead, he silently took the ladder out of the concession stand and watched her stack popcorn cups next to a square glass popcorn popper. He took in a breath, and waited for her to answer his question.

Glancing up, she sighed. "Beau says I need a new alternator." A little pout quivered on her lip as she unpacked some salt and oil from a box. "And my piston rings are worn."

Micah shook his head. "Sounds like you're going to need a complete engine rebuild before long."

She bit her lip, presumably to suppress the pout.

He turned his head, doubting she'd be doing that if she knew the sensation that shot through him at the sight.

"Beau says he can just replace the alternator now and get me back on the road."

Trying not to dwell on how much he wanted to push back the stray hairs that hadn't quite made it into her ponytail this morning, he set the ladder up on the outside of the booth. "And what about the engine?"

A side tip of her head gave her a sweetly vulnerable appearance. "I guess I'll cross that bridge when I come to it."

"Better hope your car doesn't break down right in the middle of that bridge and cause a major traffic backup." He placed a hand on a roll of gold plastic-coated fabric on the counter, and looked at the overhang above. "This go up there?"

"Yeah. That's Andra's Golden Pear Catering banner."

Taking hold of the roll, he started up the ladder. "Look on the bright side." He hooked the banner to some pegs that protruded from the overhang. "With a little focus and a lot of practice, you and Owen could walk away with the team roping championship."

She frowned. "What's that got to do with—"

"Then your engine problem becomes *my* problem. I'd be the one stuck on that bridge with other drivers cursing at me."

That cute little pout returned, only this time the eyes above it held a glint of misgiving. "I thought you said if you lost you'd fix my truck and drive *it*."

"Yeah." He climbed down again. "I thought that too till I looked under the hood."

"And?"

"It's nothing but rust."

Her face fell. "No guts, huh?"

"None worth resuscitating." Now that he was back on her level and looking her in the eye, the urge to draw a finger down her cheek was tough to ignore. "Needless to say, I'm highly motivated to win. I don't want to be saddled with that car of yours for who knows how long."

"Motivated to *win?*" A match lit behind those pretty, mistrusting eyes. "Are you deaf? How many times do I have to say it? I am not competing in—"

"That *is* Micah Brody. I told you!"

Their attention was diverted by two kids, a boy of about

ten and a girl of about eight. Brother and sister, if he had to guess.

Micah gave Janessa a look that said *I'm sorry. This will only take a second.* In the past, he'd assumed that women were impressed when fans had interrupted. But with Janessa, he needed to make sure she knew their conversation was important to him. That was just one way his eyes had been opened over the past few days.

As the kids scurried up to him, he flipped on his rodeo-guy smile. "Hey, there."

"You're Micah Brody." The boy turned calflike eyes up to him. "The bull-riding hero."

"I wouldn't say I'm a 'hero.' At least not to *some* people." He gave Janessa a look, which won him a good-natured eye roll.

"But you ride horses and you've won all kinds of awards, right?" The girl's little cheeks looked like a couple of polished apples.

"I guess that's true. You like horses?"

Both their faces lit up and they nodded.

"You have one?"

The faces fell, and the girl answered. "We don't have money for one. And our yard's too small."

"Oh." He knelt down to meet her, eye level. "Do you ever get to ride?"

They shook their heads.

"Our mom says we need all our money for food and stuff." The boy sounded like he was trying hard to accept this fact but wasn't quite there yet.

Micah looked up at Janessa, whose eyes brimmed with concern. "Well, food and stuff is important, too."

Just then, a wild-eyed woman in jeans and a paint-spattered T-shirt appeared at the top of the stairs. Her eyes darted around, then landed on the kids. She blew out a groan. "There you two are."

Micah straightened as she approached.

"I'm so sorry," she said. "I told them they could try to meet you, but I didn't mean for them to—"

"It's all right," he assured her.

The boy continued. "Our mom told us we could either spend our money on carnival rides or the rodeo, and we told her the rodeo on account of the competition being so important." He looked up at Janessa for the first time, admiration and shyness in his eyes. "All our friends are talking about it."

Clearly embarrassed, the mom allowed Micah to autograph a couple of napkins from Janessa's stand for the kids, then hustled them away.

As Janessa trailed them with her gaze, Micah eyed her, grateful for the opportunity the kids had innocently afforded him. He made a little show of shaking his head. "It's going to be awfully sad to disappoint those kids."

"You won't have to." Janessa regarded him from under an arched brow. "You're the big celebrity, not me."

He tilted a downward glance. "If you cancel, I have to cancel, too."

"Why?"

He shrugged. "I can only compete if you do. That was the deal."

"That might be the deal *you* agreed to, but not me." She started to tidy up her counter, but her eyes fixed on the livestock floor below.

He followed her gaze down to where the woman and her kids were headed toward some buckets that had been set up for painting the screen wall.

Janessa spoke softly. "I've seen that woman working

the checkout in the drugstore. I got the impression that she's a single mom."

"Oh?" His heart went out to those kids. He knew as well as anybody what it felt like to only have one parent.

"She's probably volunteering here today so her kids can see the movie for free." Melancholy had crept into her tone. "You know, my family's had some financial problems over the years, but I've always had my horse. I guess I took it for granted that if you want to ride your family finds a way."

He nodded. "I've always taken that for granted, too." *That and a lot of other things.*

The thought landed on his head like a bucket of cold water. He *had* taken a lot for granted. Like still being alive, for instance.

An unwelcome rush of memories hit him like a tsunami. The accident and those awful months spent getting back on his feet. The pain. The fear and confusion. Pouring out his heart to the night nurse in rehab because she was the only person who seemed to care enough to listen.

"Micah?" Janessa's concerned voice yanked him back to the present. She nodded at a point behind him.

Turning, he saw a boy of about eight shyly approaching with his dad's encouragement. Micah twisted full around and smiled down at the boy.

"Mr. Brody?" The boy's small voice held a quiver, as if he was unsure of how he'd be received.

Micah knelt closer to the boy's level. "Well, hey there." He reached up for Janessa to hand him another napkin to sign. "What's your name, son?"

"Daniel." The boy's face brightened at the encouraging reception.

The dad looked pleased. "Danny here's a big fan. He competes in mutton busting in the rodeo."

"No kidding." Micah gave Danny a look that said he

was as impressed as if the boy were a world-champion bull rider. "You ever win?"

"Sometimes." Danny nodded. "But my dad says that's not the most important part."

Micah looked at the dad, who shrugged. "I guess winning gets to be more important when it's your job, but I figure for the kids, rodeo should teach them something more than how to win." He gave Danny a slug to the arm that made him laugh. "I'm mighty proud of my boy."

For Micah, that comment went down like a bitter horse pill. He hadn't been that much older than Danny when he'd been set to compete in his first steer riding event. He'd been scared out of his wits, crying that he didn't want to do it.

"Be a man," his dad had barked, which had seemed like a strange thing to say to a kid.

He'd gone ahead and gotten on the animal, because he'd wanted to please his dad. When the chute opened and the steer took off bucking, Micah was terrified. He gripped the rope, waving his right arm in the air for balance like his dad had taught him. He held on for what felt like forever.

Then the buzzer sounded and he jumped off, hearing the crowd cheer for him. He was the happiest he'd ever been in his life. He ran to his dad, expecting him to say how proud he was.

"You weren't moving with the steer. He could have bucked you off."

The words stung the same now as they did then.

That particular memory threatened to break through the dam of cold emotional detachment he'd maintained for all these years. Years spent trying to please his dad but never being good enough.

He couldn't let that dam break. Especially not now.

He looked away, blinking, then back at Danny. "You're real lucky to have such a great dad."

The boy looked up at his dad, clearly in agreement.

After a minute or two of Danny telling Micah all his techniques for staying on the back of a sheep, he and his dad left. Micah stood, his head reeling. He didn't want Janessa to know that he'd just been knocked off the bull he'd been struggling to stay on in one way or another for the past twelve years.

Janessa said something about not needing any more help if he had other things to do, but by the time he'd fully tuned in, she'd changed the subject.

"Will I see you tonight?" Her eyes held a hopeful glint that he would have found encouraging if he hadn't been so preoccupied.

He hesitated, hoping his voice wouldn't shake if he spoke. "Oh…sure." Muttering something about helping out downstairs, he walked away. Just walked away.

He was starting to get real good at that.

Chapter 7

"This is almost as exciting as a livestock auction." Leonard's unmistakable husky baritone cut through the crowd noise.

Janessa and Andra had been so busy for the past hour that they'd barely had time to look up. Now as the guys from the Bar-G postured with their movie star sunglasses and their thumbs hooked in their belt loops à la Gary Cooper, Janessa admired how nicely they cleaned up.

Her pulse increasing a notch, she took a quick visual inventory. Next to Leonard stood Hank, Jimmy and Liam. She frowned. Micah must be lagging behind with Owen.

"What can we get for you fellas?" Andra, who was normally very self-assured, suddenly went a little pink-cheeked.

Janessa shrugged that off as Hank, looking remarkably like a young Clint Eastwood, made a big show of removing his shades.

"Got any buffalo bourguignonne?"

Janessa and Andra drew back at his surprisingly well-articulated query.

"Actually," Janessa responded. "We decided not to go quite so upscale."

"Okay." He nodded. "I'll just have a hot dog."

As Andra took the rest of their order, Janessa waited for the next patrons in line to decide between the Caulfield Cooler, the Bijou Punch or the Montana Mocktail. Her gaze drifted past them to the mass of moviegoers scurrying around the exhibition area. As far as she could see, Micah wasn't among them.

The bad feeling that had gnawed at her ever since he'd left that morning expanded into something she could no longer ignore. Something had triggered his mood shift, and she couldn't help but wonder if it had something to do with his apparently going AWOL after his accident. There was definitely more to this guy than met the eye.

Taking a couple of the cake pops from the popcorn tub she'd carefully filled with tissue-paper-dotted floral foam earlier in the day, she scanned the crowd one more time.

"What are you looking for?" Andra asked slyly. "Or should I say who?"

She handed the cakes to a couple of her riding students, then responded to Andra. "Oh. Nothing."

"Uh-huh. I'll let you know if I spot 'nothing' in the crowd."

She gave Andra a look. At least she could always count on having her around to understand how she felt.

"Can we save you ladies a couple of seats?" Even though Hank looked at them both, it was clear that the question was directed at Andra.

Janessa started to answer that they had planned to just watch from up there, but Andra cut her off.

"That would be great, Hank."

Janessa frowned at the higher-than-normal pitch to her friend's voice. Suddenly, it dawned on her why Andra had looked uncharacteristically nervous when the guys had shown up, and why Hank had spent the whole day carting cupcakes and popcorn tubs in his truck.

She sighed. So much for always having her best friend around.

As Hank tipped his hat and followed the rest of the guys to the stairs, Janessa jabbed Andra in the ribs. Andra gave her an innocent look, then grabbed the overly full trash can and tied up the bag with the speed and expertise of a champion tie-down roper.

"I'm just going to run this out to the Dumpster. We'll close up when I get back and go find our seats, okay?"

Wiping her hands on a towel, Janessa nodded.

As Andra hurried off, Janessa spotted Owen in the dwindling crowd. She called out to him.

His face brightening, he wove his way to the stand. "Well, hey, Janessa." He looked sheepish. "I suppose you want to talk about practicing our roping."

"Not right now." She waved that away. "You want a hot dog? I still have a couple left."

"Sounds good."

Grabbing a paper plate, she composed her words. "You here on your own?"

His face dropped like a soufflé. "No date, if that's what you mean."

Actually, that possibility hadn't even occurred to her. She cradled the hot dogs in a couple of buns, then placed them in two of the wrappers she and Andra had made to look like tiny tuxedoes. "I thought you might be here with…the other guys."

"Yeah, I'll probably sit with them." His eyes lit up as

she set the plate on the counter in front of him. "I would have ridden in with them, but I was waiting on Micah. He was out riding forever and when he finished, he said he just wanted to stay home."

"Oh?" Disappointment sat in the back of her throat like cough syrup that wouldn't quite go down. "What made him change his mind?"

Owen shrugged, handing Janessa a couple of bills. "I don't know. He was real quiet all afternoon."

The lights started to flash, and the hum of conversation grew to an enthusiastic cheer. Owen looked like he was about to go, and she blurted out the only question she could get a grip on.

"Has he said anything about the dinner he's making tomorrow?"

"Oh, yeah." Owen smiled. "He promised us the best dinner we've ever had at the bunkhouse. We're all looking forward to it." He took a step back as the lights flickered again. "Well, I should be finding the fellas." He held up his plate. "Thanks for dinner."

Janessa gave him a distracted smile. "Enjoy the movie."

Shutting off the fryer and the heat lamp, she thought about what Owen had said. Something had upset Micah enough to make him change his plans about coming to the movie. What was going on?

Andra appeared again, looking anxiously over her shoulder at the movie audience. "Come on. We should get to our seats."

"Actually," Janessa looked around and reached for an empty box. "I'm going to run a load of stuff to your car. Save us some time later." A plan formed in her head as she reached out her hand. "Can I have your keys?"

"Okay..." Andra gave her a suspicious frown. "But you might not be able to find us once they turn off the lights."

"That's okay. I'd rather just watch from up here anyway. You go on and find Hank."

Andra opened her mouth in an obvious intended objection that quickly dwindled to a dreamy grin.

After Andra had beaten a hasty retreat, Janessa looked around at the near-empty exhibition area. A chant had started to rise from the audience down below.

All at once, she knew what she had to do. She grabbed a napkin and scribbled out a note.

Andra, I borrowed your car. Please tell my mama not to worry. I'll be back after the movie.

She left the note on the counter, weighed down by a napkin holder, then headed for the stairs, hoping no one would stop her before she hit the exit.

As she slipped quietly out the door, she shot up a quick prayer. *God, please make sure I know what I'm doing!*

Micah paced the bunkhouse living room like an untamed horse penned in a corral. Not even a full day of work and a long horseback ride had put to rest the dark giants of the past that had been stirred up that morning.

Crossing to the window, he stared out at the little front yard and rubbed his hands against his temples. He'd planned on going to the movie with the guys, but for the first time since he could remember, he wasn't up to putting on his "public" face. For years, he'd thrived on being the center of attention, but now he just wanted to be alone.

That wasn't entirely true. He did want to be with Janessa.

Of course, after he'd run out on her so abruptly that morning, she most likely wouldn't want to be around him anyway. Why had he done that? She didn't expect him to put on a show, the way everyone else did. He could be himself around her. Trouble was, he'd spent so much time being what everybody else expected, he didn't even know who he was anymore.

The air in the room started to get heavy. Running his hands down his face, he moved to the front door and threw it open so he could catch a good breath. Those giants were awake all right, and staring him down, giving him no choice but to face them head-on.

And facing them meant dealing with his dad.

He shut his eyes, pushing back the whole slew of emotions brought on by that thought. Guilt. Anger. Regret. For years, all they'd had was each other. Each other, the thrill of the rodeo, and the fans. Now they were left without any of it. And in spite of all the pain his dad had caused him over the years, he had to admit that he missed him.

Remorse burned in his throat. It wasn't too late. He could still go back. Pick up right where he'd left off. Maybe even figure out a way to keep the good parts but dispense with the bad.

He rubbed his eyes. Who was he kidding? The good and the bad were interwoven as sure as the fibers in a saddle blanket.

His body started to shake and a pressure in his head pushed at his eyes and his throat. He stumbled to the bathroom, turned on the faucet and leaned down, splashing his face as if that might freeze out his feelings. It didn't work. Leaving behind his dad had only reignited the grief they'd been running from in the first place.

He leaned on the counter as distant memories popped in his brain like firecrackers. Warnings that this would happen. That he would eventually cry after his mom passed.

He had waited, looking to his dad for his emotional cues, but not seeing any. Just a dullness that settled in the places where joy and humor had once been, robbing his dad of his ability to be there for his son.

No tears had come for either of them, as far as Micah knew. Not at the funeral. Not when they'd boxed up Mom's things. Or when they'd packed their own stuff and left the house for good. Eventually, so much time passed that it had seemed pointless to want to let out the emotions. So he had kept his feelings boxed up like the dresses they'd dumped at the Goodwill on their way out of town.

Sorrow churned in his gut as he remembered his first competition, not long after. Wearing the fancy fringed shirt his mom had sewn for him that last Christmas, he'd felt small, unsteady and unsure. He hadn't wanted to compete. Hadn't shared his dad's confidence in his ability to win. Now, deep in his heart, he was still just that scared little boy, no matter how many championships he'd claimed.

The pounding of his own pulse grew deafening. He saw now why he had appreciated the attention of the buckle bunnies over the years. They made him feel loved, even though he knew it wasn't real. They were just a quick fix until he hit the next town and started to get lonely again. They were nothing but a fleeting shadow of what it had felt like to have someone in his life who really cared about him.

Straightening, he met his own reddened eyes in the mirror, hating the person behind those eyes. He shook his head. If Mom could see the man he had become, she'd be so disappointed.

Overtaken by the anguish that accompanied that realization, he gave in to a mournful wail that sounded like a tormented animal. Hot torrents of grief poured down his face, and heaving sobs surged from his throat.

Feeling frantic and trapped, he dropped to his knees, something he hadn't done in a very long time. In fact, he hadn't prayed in so long, he wasn't sure he remembered how.

"Oh, Lord." He heard a voice that sounded small and

weak, barely recognizable as his own. This must be what people meant when they talked about crying out to God.

He swallowed past the lump of grief in his throat. "Why did You take away the one person who loved me? You left me with a dad who couldn't even tell me he was proud of me." He choked out a sob. "I tried so hard to be the best. I'm a *champion.* Why wasn't that enough for him?"

He slumped against the wall with his head in his hands. This was about as low as he had ever sunk in his life. There was pretty much no hope for him.

Pulling in a jittery breath, he raised his eyes. God had to be up there somewhere beyond that dusty old glass light fixture. "Please give me some slack, God, because I'm at the end of my rope."

A dim memory faded in and out, like someone running toward him in a fog. Gradually, it became clearer. Something he'd learned a long time ago but had only thought he understood.

Do not boast except in the Lord.

He knew that, didn't he? He had worked hard in the rodeo, sure. But it had been wrong for him to take all the glory for himself. Why had that never been clear to him before those weeks in the hospital?

"Please forgive me, God." He looked up again, blinking back the moisture from his eyes. "I'm ready to live my life for You now." His voice was barely louder than his thoughts. "Make me a new man, because believe me, the old one ain't worth much."

A knock on the front door nearly launched him out of his hide.

"Micah…"

His stomach bucked at the sound of Janessa's sweet voice coming from the other room. *What on earth...?*

Clambering to his feet, he remembered he'd left the

front door open. But she was supposed to be at the movie. What was she doing here?

"Just a minute," he called out, grabbing a towel to wipe his face. He exited the bathroom and walked slowly down the short hallway and into the living room.

She stood there on the porch, eyeing him guardedly and holding two huge canvas bags. The sight of her in khaki pants that showed off her slim form, and a red T-shirt that made her dark brown hair look even richer, rustled up a spark of optimism that he hadn't felt in a very long time.

Part of him wanted to run, to leave her there with no explanation. Instead, he combed a hand through his wet-tipped hair, clinging to some crazy notion that he could still come across as cool to the only woman who had ever caught him crying.

He cleared his throat. "Well, hey, Janessa. What brings you here?"

When she didn't answer, it occurred to him that he'd better explain mighty quick why he looked like he'd just been dragged through a desert. "I would have gone to the movie, but I…" He pushed the words out of a throat still thick with emotion. "Wasn't feeling too great."

"Oh." The edge of suspicion seemed to soften into concern. "Are you sick?"

He managed a slight smile. "I'm better now."

She nodded, then lifted up the bags. "Do you feel like eating?"

He furrowed his brow. "You brought me dinner?"

"In a way. I thought you might like a little help with the meal you're making tomorrow, so I brought you a cooking lesson."

Relief and gratitude washed through him. He did need help with the dinner, but he had needed more than just that. He had needed her to show him she cared.

"But..." He took a step toward her. "I thought you were going to the movie."

She shrugged. "I thought so, too, but it turned out I wasn't in the mood." One brow arched and her eyes traced the rim of the doorway. "Are you going to invite me in?"

Moving to her, he swept a welcoming arm in front of him. As she entered, he took one of the bags. "What all have you got in here?"

She opened the bag she still held. "A bunch of stuff I grabbed from our pantry. I'm going to teach you how to make beef Stroganoff." She flashed one of the prettiest smiles he'd ever seen, then started for the kitchen, speaking over her shoulder. "There's enough here for your lesson, and I'll make you a shopping list so you can get what you'll need for tomorrow."

He paused, rubbing his chin and looking at the doorway she'd disappeared through.

Something his mom had once said came to mind, about God using all kinds of things to answer prayers. He smiled. Mom would be happy to know that God could accomplish His will even by using pretty girls who knew how to rope a calf, make beef Stroganoff and show up at just the right time.

The realization that his prayer had been answered gave him a shred of hope that underneath all his unredeemed behavior, there might just be a soul worth saving.

Chapter 8

An hour or so later Janessa sat across from Micah, enjoying the meal they'd made and sharing her frustrations over the apartment search.

"I hate to say it." He ran his fork across his plate, scraping up the last of the sauce from his second helping of Stroganoff. "But it sounds to me like your future roommate's been scammed."

"Scammed?" She jarred at the suggestion. "No, she knows what she's doing..." Her voice trailed off as the possibility got her in its grip. "You really think so?"

He shrugged, picking up her empty plate and placing it on his own. "I've seen more than my share of dishonorable landlords over the years. You ask me, this guy doesn't have anything to do with that apartment complex. He most likely doesn't even live in Seattle."

The prospect sat like a rock in her stomach. "Well, how am I supposed to find out?"

"Easy. You know the name of the complex, right?" He stood and moved to a small desk that sat against the wall under the window. "Leonard leaves his laptop here for us to use. Just look it up." He retrieved the computer and set it on the table where her plate had been. "Sometimes, it's best to just get to the truth of a situation and deal with it."

"The truth will set you free." Hesitantly, she opened the computer and turned it on.

He took the plates to the counter and started to run water into the sink, then picked up the pan from the stove. "Dinner was delicious." He plucked out a noodle and popped it into his mouth. "You sure I can make this on my own tomorrow night?"

"You saw how simple it is." She kept an eye on the screen as it moved through its paces. "I used to make it for my daddy." A dull ache squeezed her chest. Earlier, when she'd surveyed the ingredients they had on hand at the house, she'd made a hurried decision. This dish was easy enough for Micah to be able to duplicate, and it was a proven man-pleaser. Now she felt a twinge of guilt, almost as if she was betraying her daddy by fixing it for Micah.

She fingered her necklace as her attention drifted back to the computer connecting to the internet. Peripherally, she was aware of Micah giving her a studied gaze as he waited for the sink to fill.

Finally, he spoke. "So you never really told me why you gave up seeing the movie to come over here and help me."

"It's not a big deal." She shrugged. "I didn't want the guys to give you a bad time about your cooking. Besides, the movie will be playing in town all summer."

In her heart, she knew her real motivation was to find out what was troubling him. Helping with the dinner was just a convenient cover, but she was nowhere near ready to admit that. It had been plain to see by his ruddy face and rumpled hair when she arrived that she'd been right to be concerned. It had pleased her to no end when his mood had improved and he'd shown himself to have a healthy appetite.

As soon as the internet connected, she typed in Cascadian Vista Apartments Seattle. Her pulse accelerating, she clicked on the top entry. A classy-looking website popped up, featuring the words Cascadian Vista—Luxury Living in Seattle across the top. Below that was a nighttime shot of a brightly lit building with a pool in the foreground. It looked like a mansion.

"Oh," she uttered. "I think I found it." A tiny cyclone of disappointment swirled in her gut as she felt her gourmet kitchen slipping from her grasp. It was clear from this picture alone that this place was way beyond their means.

Micah crossed the room to look over her shoulder. "*Whooee.* That's some place."

"Uh-huh. Two bedrooms, two baths..." Her voice shook as she read. "Twenty-five hundred a month!" She stared at the figure. "Hana must have misunderstood. Or maybe he quoted her the price for a one bedroom."

"I don't think so." He turned the chair next to her around, sat on it backward and pointed a little lower down on the page. "It looks like the smallest unit they have is one bedroom and it goes for fourteen hundred. It's hard to mistake that for five hundred."

Janessa's mind raced. Even if they could manage to live together in a one bedroom, the thought of which made her a little queasy, that was still twice what they'd agreed they could afford. She groaned. "I really wanted this place."

"I'm so sorry." He put a hand on her shoulder. "I know how it feels to have something important fall through."

Suddenly, she was staring at the screen but not really seeing it. None of it mattered. Not the Puget Sound view or the movie room, the free Wi-Fi or even the granite countertops. All that mattered was the sensation of his hand touching her shoulder and his nearness to her.

Her pulse fluttered in her throat and all thoughts flitted from her mind. Angling her head, she met his gaze. She swallowed hard, trying to remember what they'd been talking about before her attention had been shanghaied by two pools of blue glistening with streaks of silver. She blinked, and the room started to spin.

Micah must have felt it too because he broke their gaze, then pulled his hand away. "I'm, uh...sorry about the apartment."

Right. The apartment.

Jolted back into the moment, she covered her face with her hands. "What am I going to do? I need a place to live."

He let out a long breath. "Well, I don't know about that, but I do have an idea. Something I like to do whenever I need to clear my head."

She eyed him warily. "Okay..."

He nodded toward the door. "Come on."

She never would have admitted it to him, but at that moment he could have gotten her to follow him just about anywhere.

As she headed toward the barn with Micah, she ventured a question. "You said you grew up on a ranch, too. What was it like?"

"Well, our house was scarcely bigger than the bunkhouse of the Bar-G." He cast a glance over his shoulder. "But it was home, and a great place to grow up."

She smiled. She had started to think of him like a wild horse. If she wanted to know more, she'd have to gain his trust.

As they entered the barn, Miss Molly nickered a gentle

greeting. Janessa veered toward her stall while Micah headed for the tack room.

"What do you have in mind, cowboy?" Ohh…that had sounded way less flirtatious in her head. Wincing, she rubbed Molly's soft muzzle.

"Hold your horses." He emerged from the tack room carrying a couple of coiled ropes.

Her lips spread in a slow smile. She gave Molly an extra pat and followed Micah to the corral behind the barn.

As he headed toward the steer dummy they kept out there, she smiled again. "This is where I like to come when I need to think something through. I can't believe you thought of this."

"You know what they say about 'great minds.'" He handed her one of the ropes. "Ladies first."

As she coiled her rope, thoughts of the rodeo and how she wasn't going to be in it tumbled around in her head like a litter of puppies. Now that the real cost of living in Seattle had smacked her squarely between the eyes, it was clear that she'd have to spend every minute she had focusing on earning what she needed. Not to mention that her car was going to demand a big chunk of her savings, and she still owed her half of the money Hana had been scammed out of.

She sighed. It couldn't hurt to blow off some steam by tossing a rope with the guy, but afterward, she'd have to make sure he understood that she was out.

She swung the rope, easily catching the neck of the fake steer.

"Not bad." He looked impressed. "Who taught you how to rope, anyway?"

"My daddy." She crossed to the dummy to retrieve her line. "I begged him to teach me everything there was to know around the ranch because I loved being with him so much."

"Sounds like you were a daddy's girl." The words came out glazed with admiration.

"He was the best. I used to cook for him, and he'd pretend to be a customer in my restaurant. We loved that game." It felt surprisingly easy to share that memory, considering that she never really talked about Daddy, not even with Mama or Andra.

"You know—" he gave her a studied gaze before throwing his loop "—you've been worrying that necklace to a nub ever since I met you. Why is that?"

She glanced down at her simple diamond on a heavy gold chain that she hadn't even realized she had her fingers on. "My daddy gave this to me on my last birthday before he died." That final word sputtered out, barely audible.

His gaze drifted past her, as if her words had prompted a painful thought of his own.

"I always wear it." Forced cheerfulness was a skill she'd honed over the years. "It's my birthstone."

He blinked, seemingly drawn back to the conversation. "I figured it looked like it was made for a kid."

"It was." She built the loop in her rope again. "I was eight when he gave it to me."

"And how did he..." He allowed the question to hang in the air, finding its own completion.

"Cancer." She swung again, this time twirling her rope in an ocean wave and catching the horns with a figure eight. She yanked it tight. "I still can't really talk about it. But it's like they say, life goes on."

She went over to grab her loop, then looked back at him. While he nodded approval at her roping, the melancholy returned to his eyes. She frowned, realizing that in everything she'd read about him, there'd been no mention of his mom. Only his dad.

She measured her words. "I guess maybe you know about that, too."

"Yeah." He gave a quick, sad smile, maintaining his focus on his rope. "My mom died of lupus when I was ten."

Her heart broke for him. Aside from Adam, she really hadn't met anyone else who'd lost a parent so young. "I'm so sorry."

His mouth twisted as he did an impressive series of tricks and swung the rope over the horns. "Life goes on, like you said." His expression firmed in a way that she recognized from her own arsenal of survival techniques. "My dad never said it, but I think he blamed God for my mom dying, so that's what I did, too. The two of us just hit the road, me riding in the rodeo and him helping with the animals. We never looked back."

"Wow. It must have been hard having to leave your home like that."

"Home's pretty important." He glanced over at her before retrieving his rope. "Can I ask you a question?"

"Sure."

"Why are you so dead set against staying in Thornton Springs?"

The question took her by surprise. Why would he want to know? "It's just…small towns. You get stuck in them and your life goes nowhere. Don't you ever feel that way?"

"I haven't stayed in one place long enough to feel stuck."

"Oh. Well, trust me, that's what happens."

"And you think things would be different if you lived in a city."

"Cities are so much more exciting." As she spoke, she mimicked the rope tricks he'd just demonstrated. "My parents used to take us to Spokane with them in the summers.

I loved walking down the streets there and looking in the windows of the restaurants. They just seemed so special to me." She jumped into her loop, pulled it up over her head, then tossed it over the horns. Flicking him a *how-about-that* glance, she went to the steer.

"Nice roping, cowgirl."

A blush found her neck. *Now* who was sounding flirtatious?

Recoiling her rope, she walked back to where he stood. "I always loved seeing the people sitting at those perfect little tables, looking like they were having the time of their lives. I wanted to be a part of that."

"So you decided to become a chef."

She nodded. "I'd always come home from those trips wanting to learn to cook new things. Daddy loved seeing me so happy. *That's* why I want to be a chef."

An eyebrow quirked as he focused on twirling his lasso. "And you have to move to a city to do that?"

"I don't know. There's just something exciting about the idea of living in a city. The pace. The energy. The way people have more to talk about than heifer checks and ag stats. Besides, that dream made my daddy happy."

That look of unwavering certainty that Janessa had found so galling just a few short days ago came over him. "You ever think maybe it wasn't the details that made him happy?"

Something tugged in her gut. "What do you mean?"

"I mean, did you ever consider that maybe what pleased him was the idea of you doing something you loved? The dream could change, it was the result that he liked."

Defensiveness swirled around her like the lasso he kept twirling, but before she could get a good enough grip to swing it around his know-it-all neck, she stopped. Maybe he was right.

Turning his attention back to the steer dummy, he swung and spoke again. "Sounds like your daddy was a real good man."

She smiled sadly, her defensiveness subsiding. "The best. When he died, I just couldn't help thinking, why him? We needed him so much. My mama worked so hard for all those years, just to become a widow at forty-two. It just didn't seem fair."

He nodded, his mouth rising in a slight smile. "Oh, I get it now."

"Get what?"

"Why you're so determined not to get married."

The remark caught her off guard. A well-thought-out retort burbled up her throat, but all that made it out was a pathetic, "W…why?"

"You're afraid that if you find somebody as great as your daddy, you'll just lose him, too."

Her head snapped up. "No. That's not true…" *Was it?*

She jutted out her chin. This was supposed to be all about his deep, dark past. Why were they dredging up hers?

She let her rope drop, just to give her hands something to do by recoiling it. "Is that the way *you* feel? About your mama?"

He shook his head sadly. "I wouldn't deserve someone like her."

She looked away, not wanting to dwell on the implications of his last statement, then swung her rope again, fumbling for anything to change the subject. "What about your dad? Is he still around?"

He shifted uncomfortably, his eyes darkening. "Oh, yeah. He's around."

"You sound like you don't know where he is."

"I knew where he was when I left him. Honestly, I don't really care."

His words hung heavy like a curtain about to part, revealing the rest of his story. Now that she was close, she wasn't so sure she wanted to know.

She proceeded with care. "Why did you leave?"

He shook his head. "It's complicated. We've got a lot of water under the bridge, him and me."

Realizing that this might be her only opportunity, she rustled up her nerve. "I read about your accident."

He paused, then continued. "What'd you read?"

"Just that it happened. You had a bad round and got kicked by the bull." She paused, feeling awkward at having said it. "They say it's the most dangerous sport in the world. I guess that's right, huh?"

His jaw firmed. "There's more to it than they printed in the papers. It wasn't just an accident."

Her stomach pitched. "What do you mean?"

He looked off in the distance for a long moment, then tipped his head toward a hay bale a few feet away. They sat, and she heard him take in a long breath.

"We were at a rodeo in Amarillo. I won my first round, but my second round I didn't do so well. I drew a Brahma bull named Easy who was having a better night than I was. He threw me on the second buck—all of me but my left hand, which got hung up in the rope. That happens sometimes."

She gave a sympathetic nod.

"Trouble was, while the bullfighters were helping me get loose, Easy decided he had somewhere better to be. He took off, bent on severing the relationship between me and my arm. By some miracle, my hand got loose and I pumped my arms in the air to let the crowd know I was okay, but I realized right away I wasn't." He ran a hand down his arm. "I've sprained my shoulder lots of times, but this was different. Downright excruciating. The doctor told me it was broken and I figured I'd be out for a while. That's a tough blow for a bull rider."

She rolled in her lips. She'd never been a fan of that event for that very reason. It was so dangerous.

"Anyway, my dad was right there in the emergency room with me, and as soon as the doctor left, he started in on me about everything I had done wrong in the ring that night. He said how I had to ride the third round the next day. How I needed to 'cowboy up' and 'be a man.'"

"But your shoulder was broken. How did he expect you to hang on?"

He shrugged. "'A real man would work through the pain.' I'd been hearing it for years. I didn't expect any sympathy from him." He paused. "Anyway, the stock contractors typically save their meanest bulls for the last day, so—no surprise—I drew Texas Tornado, a rank bull with a grudge against humanity. Normally, that wouldn't worry me, but I wasn't exactly at my best. And I guess you know how that went."

"I read that you made it to the buzzer." That was impressive. Most riders couldn't claim that achievement on a rank bull, the toughest of the tough.

"I honestly don't remember those eight seconds. I felt a little sick, on account of I was hanging on with my bad arm." He patted his shoulder. "All I wanted was to get off and put some distance between me and Texas Tornado. The second I heard the buzzer, I jumped off. I felt both feet hit the ground, but something happened. My vision got foggy and I couldn't move. I hesitated just long enough for him to decide to play El Toro with me."

She bit her lower lip, not sure if she wanted to hear the rest.

He gave a long blink before going on. "I really don't remember this part, but my dad showed it to me on the tape. So I could 'learn from it.' In those couple of seconds that I stood there wavering, I guess Texas Tornado saw me as an easy target. He charged, and tossed me in the air like a pitchfork full of hay."

She pulled in a gasp.

"And he didn't stop there. Maybe he wanted to take revenge on behalf of all his bullring ancestors, I don't know, but he pretty much did a flamenco dance on my backbone before calling it a day."

A hot tear pooled in her eye and she reached up to swipe it away. Reading about this had seemed less real. Now she just wanted to wrap her arms around him and tell him it was all going to be okay.

"The next thing I knew—" his voice had lowered to just above a whisper "—I woke up in the hospital with a fractured spine that was an inch short of killing me."

"Oh, Micah." She reached over, adapting her wished-for hug into an amicable touch to his upper arm. "That never would have happened if your dad hadn't shamed you into riding with a broken shoulder."

He nodded sadly. "If I hadn't been trying to please him, I would have made a different decision. As it was, I thought I was invincible. But, I learned a lesson that day I'll never forget."

Pulling back her hand, she hugged herself to ward off the evening chill.

"That night in the hospital, I had an epiphany. Under the fog of the pain meds, years of Sunday school lessons came back to me. I realized I was doing it all on my own strength, getting too full of myself and taking the glory for my success."

That caught her attention. She had to admit, she'd secretly planned to keep an eye out for him in the congregation on Sunday to see if he was a churchgoer.

He let out a jagged breath. "Once I checked out of rehab, I knew I couldn't go back to the way things were. Trouble is, without the rodeo, I don't even know who I am."

She felt numb. They just sat for a minute, breathing in the scent of dust mingled with sweet hay, and staring out to where the sun had just dipped below the smoky blue mountains.

"So," she said finally, "how did you wind up here?"

He kept his gaze distant, as if the answers to life's hard questions might be spelled in the sea of waving yellow grass in front of them.

"I just headed toward Montana, because it was the only place I'd ever called home. At a truck stop in Wyoming, I overheard some guys talking about a ranch in Thornton Springs that was looking for a man. I figured that would at least keep me busy while I figured out what to do with my life. When I got here, it almost felt like going back to our little ranch in Havre. To the last time in my life when I really remembered being *happy*."

The honesty of that admission felt painful in its intensity.

"And then I met you." His gaze locked onto hers. "And you really *got* to me."

"I got to you?" Her stomach fluttered. "What do you mean?"

"When you goaded me about the rodeo, I started to think maybe I could handle it this time. Maybe I could learn not to take credit for my skill. To give it to God and let Him work His will, just like my mom would have said. That's why I signed us up for the rodeo. I thought it was for Owen and Keely, but now I realize it was mostly my chance to try to make amends with God."

The blood drained from her face. She'd been right all along. This competition *was* about Micah, but not in the way she'd thought. It wasn't that he was trying to show off. He was trying to prove something to himself.

Her earlier resolve fell away like dry flower petals. She'd been trying to tell him she couldn't compete because of the school that apparently didn't even want her. To force her own will on a situation that was beyond her control.

In that moment, she let go of the dream of attending Le Cordon, and it was okay. It had to be. She was giving it over to God, and clearly God had other plans. Micah needed her. She couldn't let him down.

She bumped his knee with hers, then stood, taking a few steps and preparing her loop.

He looked up at her, his eyes questioning.

"So..." She swung her rope and gave him a taunting smile. "Are you going to just sit there, or are you going to teach me everything you know about roping?" She tossed the loop at him, making an easy catch around his shoulders, and pulled the rope taut.

Laughing, he allowed her to draw him to his feet. "Looks to me like you've mastered the basics." He gave the rope a quick tug, reeling her in like a lake trout.

She let out a gasp as she collided with his firm chest.

Looking down at her, he dented that gorgeous dimple. "Now what do you say we get to some serious roping?"

Chapter 9

An interesting thing happened to Micah as the weeks went by. Thornton Springs started to feel like home.

Six mornings a week, he and Owen got up earlier than the other guys to do roping drills, slowly making headway on Owen's skills. After a long day of hard but gratifying ranch work, they'd head out for more practice, usually with Keely and Janessa. After almost five weeks of training, Micah was pleased and impressed with all three of his pupils.

Even after all this time, he hadn't quite figured Janessa out. Considering her initial objections to participating in the rodeo, she'd suddenly become surprisingly available for practice. He'd tried not to get his hopes up, but when they were together, they reminded him of Angela Bijou and Jeffrey Mark Caulfield in that movie they'd finally gone to with Owen and Keely, one night after a particularly productive practice. It was as though they had a total, inexplicable ease with each other.

Now, the night before the rodeo, as the two of them sat on the cow print seats of a booth at Moo, platonically eating ice cream, he tried to keep his focus on the conversation, which had naturally turned once again to the rodeo.

"You nervous about tomorrow?" He licked the last bit of rocky road from the bottom of his cone.

"More like excited. Owen's gotten really consistent. It was a good idea you had for us to practice in front of the guys. I think that helped him get over his stage fright."

"They're pretty supportive. And they think the world of Owen."

"They seem pretty fond of you, too." She took a bite of bubblegum, which he had quickly figured out was her favorite ice cream. "I noticed they've pegged you with a nickname, Emeril."

"I have you to thank for that. They think I'm a regular chef. I told them I got some mighty good training, better than any school could've given me."

Her smile dimmed, and he was instantly sorry he'd said it. "I didn't mean to—"

"It's fine." She held up a hand. "I've totally accepted that I'm not going to Le Cordon. Not this year, anyway. I can always try again next year, and in the meantime, at least I'll be living in Seattle. I can get a restaurant job and start applying to community colleges."

"I'm real sorry." And he really *was* sorry. Sorry that she hadn't gotten into her school, but even more so that she was leaving town anyway.

He shifted in his seat as reality kicked him in the side with a sharp spur. Janessa's time here was almost up. Tomorrow, the rodeo would come and go, and the string of long evenings in the corral with her would have come to an end.

"It's okay." She smiled over at him. "It's actually a relief in a way. Without the pressure of paying for such an expensive school, I've been able to ease up on my work schedule."

"Oh, so that explains it." He tried not to let on that a sadness had engulfed him.

"Explains what?"

"Why you suddenly had time to practice with us. Why you decided to compete in the rodeo after all."

"Yes." She smiled and blushed, an appealing combination. "I guess that explains it."

If she had been any other woman, he would have taken her look to have an unspoken meaning. Janessa wasn't really that kind of girl. If she wanted you to know how she felt about something, she pretty much told you. At least, that was what he'd observed. But part of him, the wannabe one-woman-kind-of-guy part of him, hoped he wasn't entirely right about that.

He derailed that train of thought before it could reach the part of the track where the bridge between his manly ego and his ability to sell himself had been washed out. She was still planning on leaving. Any attraction she might have for him wasn't enough to persuade her to revise that plan.

"So," he said quietly. "You have a place lined up to live yet?"

She rolled those beautiful eyes. "Not exactly. Once I told Hana that we found out the apartment ad was a fake, she took about a week to accept it, then another week to readjust her thinking to a realistic price range. She's still unemployed, so I think she's shifted her focus to her job hunt. The only other place she's found so far turned out to be a studio."

"It's not too late to change your plans."

"I can't back out of our agreement. Not when she's done so much work on the apartment search."

"I think your loyalties might be a little misguided."

"Could be." She consulted her watch. "Hey, if we're going to find my family before the parade starts, we'd better get a move on."

A minute later, they stepped out to the sidewalk, which was bustling with folks jockeying for parade-viewing positions.

Janessa pointed across the street. "Mama said they set up their chairs in front of the feed store."

As they started to walk, an unexpected wave of anxiety hit. He tried to sound casual. "So, you like parades?"

"I love them. I always get excited about the carnival, too."

"I'm glad to hear that." He reached into his pocket and pulled out the red paper strip he'd acquired earlier from Danita, who was giving discounts on haircuts with the purchase of ride tickets. "Because I'm going to need a little help getting these used up."

She laughed that joyful laugh that he'd grown to relish. Over the past weeks, he'd found himself calculating ways to make her laugh whenever possible just so he could enjoy the sound.

They made their way toward the feed store, stopping several times to greet people they knew. Everyone in town seemed to recognize him now, and to call him by name. Even though rodeo mania had gripped Thornton Springs by the horns, most folks had started to treat him like he was just another resident of the town. He had to admit that he preferred that to the adoration.

Now it was really only the tourists, and the females wearing those buttons proclaiming their fan club affiliation, who still acted awkward around him. For the most part, Micah had come to feel something about this town that he hadn't even known he wanted. He felt like he belonged there. He hadn't really belonged in a place since he and his dad had left Havre.

"Hello, Janessa. Micah." Pastor John and his wife Peggy waved with cotton-candy-sticky hands as they passed.

It warmed him to have a pastor greet him by name, not because he knew the danger of Micah's occupation and figured he could use a talking-to about getting right with Jesus, but because he was a bona fide member of the congregation. That was one of the biggest surprises of all to Micah about this new life he'd found.

On Sundays, he'd started going to the little church in town, first by himself—slipping in the back after service had started—then accepting Owen's invitation to sit with him and the other guys. The Greenes always sat near the front, and Janessa spotted him one time, giving him a sweet smile that spoke volumes. In that smile, Micah wanted to think he saw his mom letting him know she was pleased that, after all these years, he'd finally begun to reconnect with God.

"Don't let it go to your head," Janessa said now, leaning in so close that her shoulder brushed against his arm. "But I think you have some fans."

Micah trailed her gaze to a pair of little girls who were weaving their way through the crowd like a couple of tiny missiles.

He put his hands on his knees, and bent to their level. "Hey, Carrie. Hey, Chrissy. How's the club going?"

They chattered on in that fast-paced, overlapping way that only girls seem to understand. After they'd answered his question to their satisfaction, they said goodbye and disappeared into the market.

Janessa smirked sideways at him. "Don't tell me you have a *junior* fan club now."

"No." He laughed. "I was sitting in the diner one day and those two caught sight of me and came over to ask for my autograph."

"How unusual." She spiked the words with a playful hint of sarcasm that he pretended to ignore.

"They told me that because of me coming to town, they'd started a riding club, so all the kids from school who didn't have horses of their own could ride theirs."

"Oh…wow."

"It really got to me, so I offered to make a 'guest appearance' at their next club meeting to teach the new riders about horse safety. I have to say, it was about the most outright gratifying thing I've done in a long time."

He caught her giving him a thoughtful look. For a moment, he lost himself in the rich brown of her eyes, the shape of her face, the creaminess of her skin. He'd never been lost in another person like that before. Nowhere near.

The urge to tell her how he felt about her took him by the throat and gave him a good shake. He was in serious danger of saying something that would force her to explain why she had no interest in settling down with anyone—something that might lead her to demand the same explanation from him. Instead, he focused on her lips. A big mistake, since that caused him to lean in closer to her. Dangerously close.

"Micah Brody! Micah Brody!"

They simultaneously jerked back from each other as the two kids they'd met the day of the movie premiere, the ones who had told him they'd chosen watching him in the rodeo over going to the carnival, ran toward him like a couple of calves out of the chute.

"Well, hey, you two." He looked up to see their mom

weaving through the crowd in an only partly successful attempt at keeping up with them.

The kids chattered excitedly about how much they were looking forward to the rodeo tomorrow.

"We've been saving our car-washing money all summer." The boy beamed.

Their mom finally caught up to them, looking a little exasperated. "I told you two not to run off." She looked at Micah and Janessa. "I'm sorry. They're just so excited about the rodeo."

The girl bobbed up and down like a cork in a pond. "We've never been to one before, on account of they cost money."

The blush that crept up their mom's face wasn't lost on Micah. He looked at the kids. "Tomorrow's going to be a mighty special day for you two."

"Come on, kids." Their mom put a hand on each of their shoulders. "The parade's about to start."

Just as she began to herd them away, Carrie and Chrissy bounded out of the market with the same enthusiasm with which they'd entered it. A moment of pure inspiration hit Micah.

"Hey." He leaned down to the boy and girl. "You should talk to these girls here about joining their riding club."

The four kids instantly bonded in an animated exchange over what the club entailed, and that yes, it was completely free.

Micah looked over at the mom, whose eyes were welling. Giving Janessa a look that was only slightly apologetic, since he knew she'd understand, he reached into his pocket and took out the roll of ride tickets.

When he handed it to the mom, she looked confused, then tried to hand them back.

Micah held up his hands. "I really want you to have them."

Gratitude washed over her face as she mouthed the words, "Thank you."

As she walked away with the four kids, who were now engaged in a lively discussion about horses, Janessa turned to Micah. "That was really nice of you."

He shrugged one shoulder. "I'll bet that mom has to say no to them enough as it is. She deserves a break."

"It would have taken us all day to use those tickets anyway." She smiled.

"Hey." He jarred. The parade was about to start and he needed to get Janessa to a place where she'd be able to see. "Come on. I don't want to miss the parade."

She gave him a questioning look. He smiled to himself and guided her toward the place where her mama and Mr. Bloom sat next to Adam and Courtney in lawn chairs. He exchanged an anxious smile with Adam, hoping that this had been a good idea.

If it wasn't, it was too late now.

Janessa stood on her toes with her hands on the back of Mama's lawn chair, ultra-aware of Micah standing next to her. As they watched the rodeo royalty, antique fire trucks and kids leading livestock on leashes, her arm occasionally brushed against his, sending a jolt through her that only added to the excitement of the parade.

An earsplitting *honk* shifted her attention from the high school marching band in front of them to a string of vintage cars and trucks working its way up the street.

"Oh!" Leaning in to get a better view, she clutched at Micah's arm. "This is my favorite part!"

With a start, she realized she had unintentionally

gripped his biceps with both hands. She let go, quickly returning her hands to the safety of Mama's chair.

Much to her relief, he gave her arm a good-natured jab with his elbow. When she smiled up at him, he rewarded her with a wink that melted most of her self-consciousness and at least a little of her heart.

Oooh, boy.

As the vintage vehicles wended past, Janessa and Micah quizzed each other on their knowledge of years and models. Then she leaned forward to get a better view of a sleek-looking deep sky-blue 1949 Chevy Thriftmaster which was slowly making its way up the street in a scallop pattern.

"Micah, look!" She backhanded him playfully in the ribs. "Someone has a truck just like mine."

"Yep." He rubbed his side as if she'd wounded him. "*Just* like yours."

"Look how pretty it is." An unexpected yearning took her in its grip. She had a photo in her room of her granddaddy standing next to Old Blue back when he was young and it was new. The photo was in black and white, but this was just what she'd always pictured her truck looking like it did in its heyday.

She released a sigh. "I swear, if I could get mine restored—"

She stopped herself, thinking the driver looked an awful lot like Owen. Then as the girl in the passenger seat leaned out the window and shouted "Janessa!" she realized it was Keely. She threw her hands over her mouth.

Her family and Mr. Bloom were watching her now, as Owen honked the horn, and Keely waved her arms. The final giveaway was the banner draped across the side that read Bar-G Ranch.

She let out a scream and started jumping up and down like a kid on a pogo stick. "That's my truck!" She whooped again, then threw herself at Micah in a big hug. "I can't believe it. This is the most amazing thing anybody has ever done for me."

"Hey, it wasn't just me. Adam and Owen and Beau helped." He seemed to have no problem returning the hug. "Besides, I did it for myself, too, you know. Remember our deal? I couldn't take any chances that I might wind up driving your car. I have my reputation to consider."

Coming out of the hug she slugged his arm, then leaned down to wrap her arms around Adam. She watched the tail end of the truck for a moment, and grabbed Micah's wrist. "Come on."

"Where are we going?"

"To the end of the parade route."

"But the parade's not over."

"I don't care. I have to go see my truck." She spoke over her shoulder as they started to weave through the throng. "How did you get it running? You said it was nothing but rust."

"Easy. We put the body of the old truck onto the frame of a newer one."

"That was *easy?*"

"Okay, maybe not 'easy.' But it worked. And the guys and I had a good time."

She smiled, picturing the four of them bonding while drinking root beer and banging the dents out of Old Blue. Then, halting in her tracks, she whipped around and clutched his arm. "Hang on. Did you say you bought another truck?"

"No big deal." He attempted to keep walking, but she remained rooted.

"But, that must have cost a fortune. I can't accept that."

"Janessa." Taking hold of her shoulders, he looked at her with a seriousness that caught her breath. "I wanted to do this for you. I know you don't want to drive your truck around Seattle, but at least now it's not rusting out in the back garage anymore. Besides, you're the one who said I should do something for somebody else. I made a lot of money in the rodeo, and I want to do some giving back."

Warmth rushed over her, along with the smallest sliver of willingness to see what the future might hold with this guy. As they stood there, his eyes locked on to hers with an intensity that hinted he might be feeling the same.

"Micah, sugar!"

A blur of blond hair piled high over an artfully made-up face burst through the crowd like Texas Tornado in stiletto boots. Janessa retreated back as the woman pulled Micah into a crushing bear hug. He stood there, not participating in the hug but not exactly stopping it, either.

Who was this woman? She didn't look much older than Janessa, but her short skirt and formfitting fringed cowgirl blouse gave her a self-assured appearance that caught Janessa up in an unexpected cyclone of insecurity.

Finally, the woman stepped back, gripping Micah's upper arms with carefully manicured fingers.

"Aw, sugar. I'm so glad to see ya!" The words stretched out in a Texas drawl that was as thick as honey and at least as sweet.

Micah blinked. "Carly?"

The blonde…Carly…beamed up at him. "I knew you'd be surprised to see me!" Her gaze flipped to Janessa and the sugary smile faded to a flat red line. She held a beat, then turned back to Micah, the corners of her mouth curving up faintly. "Did ya miss me?"

Micah rubbed the back of his neck, which had mottled either from embarrassment or the intensity of the hug. Just as he was about to answer, his eye hooked on something in the crowd and his face went white.

Janessa followed his line of sight to an unfamiliar Stetson-wearing man with a slight paunch shoving his way through the parade-watchers, his eagle-eye gaze honed in on Micah.

"Dad." Micah breathed out the word barely louder than a whisper.

Janessa's heart raced. Everything he'd told her about his dad hadn't painted a very healthy picture of their relationship, and as far as she knew, Micah hadn't intended to remedy that any time soon.

"Well." The man raised his hands on approach, as if he might be expecting a hug. He cocked his head. "You don't look very happy to see me."

Looking from one man to the other, Janessa grabbed her elbows and faded back a step. Carly, on the other hand, sent a bright Texas smile to both men. Clearly, the elder Mr. Brody's presence here came as no surprise to her. What was going on?

"I don't want to talk to you right now, Dad." Speaking through clenched teeth, Micah held up both palms like a shield.

"Hey." Mr. Brody flicked Janessa a disapproving glower, then jabbed a finger at Micah's face. "We talk when I say we're going to talk."

Carly caught Janessa's eye. Subtly, her lips shifted into a smile as she eased around Micah and effectively inserted herself into the space between him and Janessa.

"So, how do y'all know Micah?" Her voice seemed friendly and conversational, but masked a curious appraisal.

Janessa squinted. The question felt oddly timed but, given Carly's proximity, she had little choice but to focus on her rather than on the barbs flying between the two men.

"I…uh…" How much did she really want to tell her? "He works at my family's ranch."

Incredulity flickered across the face that seemed disarmingly pretty under all that makeup. Then her mouth lifted and she thrust out a hand. "I'm Carly. Micah's…" The pause stretched like taffy, ending in a sticky sweet, "Good friend."

The emphasis she put on the word *friend* implied more than its conventional meaning. Janessa stared dumbly, ignoring the offer to shake.

Moving her hand to her chin, Carly studied Janessa with narrowing black-lined eyes. She tipped another glance at the men, then returned her focus to Janessa, giving the impression that she was about to stake her claim. "Listen." Her demeanor softened and, for a moment, she looked like she wanted to be genuinely helpful. "Micah needed to get away for a while. We all understand that."

She glanced over her shoulder, indicating that by "we all" she at least meant herself and Micah's dad. Janessa had to wonder who "all" else was included in that assemblage.

"He's had a really rough time. Trust me, I've been there for him through *so many* long nights when he couldn't sleep and needed to talk."

Janessa's heart slammed into her rib cage. *Been there for him? Nights when he couldn't sleep?* The implications were obvious.

Carly took on the countenance of someone about to break some really bad news. "He's goin' back to the rodeo circuit. Y'all know that, right? It's only a matter of time, and his dad is convinced that it would be best for him not to wait. I'll be handlin' his PR, so I have a vested interest in his mental mind-set." Her compassionate look suddenly turned possessive. "If y'all care about Micah and his future, y'all won't stand in his way."

Janessa flinched, wondering what Carly thought she might do to interfere with Micah's "mental mind-set."

Tilting her head, Carly gave her a compassionate look that would have been comforting under different circumstances. "I'm real sorry to have to tell ya that, darlin'."

Janessa's stomach did a cartwheel. Why should it come as any surprise that he had female "friends" who would claim him as their territory? He'd warned her that he was a "nothing serious" kind of guy but, like a fool, she'd allowed herself to get mired in the quicksand of his handsome bull-rider charm.

Heat rushed to her cheeks and she started to feel a little dizzy.

Seeing that her counsel had achieved its intended effect, Carly gave her a final look and turned her attention back to Mr. Brody's ongoing tirade.

Wrapping her arms around herself, Janessa lowered her head. Even though their argument was happening in the most public of settings, she felt like an intruder, like she should remove herself from the situation in which she had no place.

She pivoted to face the street as if the parade still held an interest. Maybe Carly was right. Obviously, Micah had some things he needed to work out with his dad, but the rodeo was his life. Maybe he really was going back.

Anger jockeyed with heartache as she tried to tune out the conversation at her back. What had she been thinking? If it hadn't been for Micah and his charisma, she would have kept up her pace at work, and she'd have the money she needed to move. She would have put time into researching apartments and jobs in Seattle, and maybe even called her school to find out why she hadn't heard from them. Now because of him she was that much further behind and, to top it all off, she felt like a complete fool.

As the tiny ballerinas from the local dance school sashayed past in their pink tutus, she pulled in a jagged breath. It wasn't entirely his fault. Sure, he had helped her with her roping and fixed up her truck, but she had been the one to take those things to mean more than just a show of friendship. He hadn't promised her anything.

Feeling a sudden surge of remorse for her anger toward him, she glanced back over her shoulder. Catching her gaze, Carly lifted a warning brow over innocent china doll eyes, then slipped her arm through Micah's. Still embroiled in the heated dispute with his dad, Micah didn't acknowledge Carly's action, but neither did he push her away. They clearly had an ease with one another that had to be the result of…what? Lots of sleepless nights spent *talking?*

Humiliation burned into Janessa's cheeks like a brand on a steer. Was fixing her truck the equivalent of "so many long nights" with girls like Carly? Did this Casanova customize his courting to fit the girl?

There *had* been more to the roping and the truck fixing than just a show of friendship. He had seen her as a challenge, like a filly he'd wanted to break. And it had almost worked.

She turned back to face the street, jarred by the sight of the big flatbed truck that a bunch of ranchers fixed up every year to look like a pirate ship. Her daddy had been one of the rancher pirates when she was little, and the abrupt reminder of him was like a tiny dagger to her heart.

If only Daddy were here to guide her through this. To give her some fatherly perspective on how men think. Was that why she had sworn off relationships? Because she'd missed out on that guidance? The thought brought a fresh gush of tears to her eyes.

Just as she clutched at her necklace for comfort, a loud *boom!* practically blasted her out of her skin. The fake cannon from the pirate ship had just showered candy into the air, and a bunch of kids lunged from behind her. The force inadvertently shoved her off balance, and as she reflexively reached out to steady herself, she felt the chain around her neck give way. In a terrible instant, she clutched at her throat to feel for her most treasured possession, but it was gone.

Panicking, she dropped to her knees. Pushing aside corn-dog wrappers and popped balloons, she bobbed her head to see through the forest of legs and the kids scurrying around picking up candy.

A dim awareness of Micah's cowboy boots next to her on the pavement and his hands on her shoulders weakened her knees but not her resolve.

"What are you doing?" The calmness of his voice only agitated her more. This was his fault—at least partly—and he was only making it worse.

"Nothing…I…" There was no sign of the necklace. An urge to go through the pockets of every one of the candy-hoarding kids in the immediate vicinity crossed her mind, but she didn't want to come across like a total lunatic.

Feeling ridiculous now, she shot to her feet, her eyes still darting around in search of her diamond.

"I'm sorry." His voice was like a distant hum in the background of her desperate thoughts. "About the interruption, I mean."

"What?" She couldn't think about that now, in light of this new problem. That necklace was her one remaining link to her daddy.

He said something about hashing things out with his dad, and she heard herself say she needed to get home. This was so silly. All she wanted was for the street to clear so she could locate her treasure, but since that wasn't going to happen, she needed to get away before she burst into tears.

Without really looking at Micah, she turned and shoved her way through the crowd. The familiar pain of loss coursed through her veins. Loss of her daddy…the neck-lace…and Micah.

But how could she feel a loss of something that had never even been hers?

She picked up her pace. Micah had Carly. What did he need her for, anyway? Now all she wanted was to get to the safety of her car and put some miles between her and the source of all her confusion.

Chapter 10

As Janessa led Miss Molly from the fairgrounds barn to the rodeo arena, her heart felt like a stone. If she hadn't been so confused the night before, she could have stayed focused until she found her most treasured possession.

But the necklace, she had to admit, wasn't the only reason her heart ached. In spite of her acceptance that she wasn't really anything special to Micah, she couldn't help but scan the faces around her in the hope of seeing him.

The area behind the stands brimmed with people pacing their horses in preparation for their events, but there was no sign of Micah. Disappointment blended with nervous relief, brewing up a mixed batch of confusion. Part of her yearned to see him, to go back to the way things had been before his dad and Miss Sweet Tea had shown up. But the more sensible side of her said it would be best to just avoid him altogether before she left for Seattle.

Not that she knew exactly when that would be, since

she had no school, job or apartment waiting for her out there. Anticipation quavered in her chest. Once she had the rodeo behind her, she'd be able to help Hana with the apartment search. That—along with figuring out what to do about the truck—was her major obstacle. Once that was taken care of, she'd be on her way.

So why wasn't she rejoicing at the thought?

She approached the fence at the edge of the arena, where the tie-down roping was in full swing. Her anticipation grew along with the clamor of the crowd, the taste of dust and the smell of nachos. It was a good thing, too, because the team-roping event was coming up in just a few minutes, and she'd have to be ready.

The stands were packed fuller than she'd ever remembered seeing them. Even though it still pinched a little that most everyone was there to watch Micah, she had to admit that his coming here had been really good for the town. Between his presence in the rodeo and the movie being shot there, Thornton Springs was experiencing a much-needed boost to its economy.

"Ness! Hey, Janessa!"

Andra's voice diverted Janessa's attention to the walkway behind her, where her friend tore through the gathering of horses and riders. She wore her hair in its usual bun, but today it was tied up with a red bandana, befitting the occasion.

"I'm so glad I found you." Andra stopped to catch her breath, then pursed her lips like she was about to make an announcement. "I know nothing can ever replace the necklace you lost…" She reached into her purse and took out a small flat box. "But I thought maybe this could represent a new phase of your life."

Puzzled, Janessa wrapped Molly's reins loosely around the top fence rung, then took the box and flicked it open.

She gasped at the stunning cross on a delicate gold chain. "Oh, Andra. It's beautiful."

"I want it to remind you that you'll always have your dad in your heart, whether you have the heart hanging around your neck or not."

A tear welled in Janessa's eye as she undid the necklace from its casing and handed the box back to Andra. "And that I'll always have Jesus with me." She fastened the chain around her neck, then clasped the cross in her fingers. "Thanks, Andra." She pulled her friend into a hug.

As Andra attempted to put her arms around her in return, her purse fell and landed in the dirt at their feet. As she knelt to retrieve it, Janessa spotted a small yellow object next to it.

"Andra!" She bent down to pick up the object, then straightened. Thrusting a hand on her hip, she presented the Micah Brody Fan Club button. "Really?"

"Oh…" Wincing, Andra snatched the button from her, shoving it back into her purse. "You weren't supposed to see that."

"You're my best friend." Janessa feigned a pout.

"I know, and I'm rooting for you, honest. It's just that…" Andra shrugged. "He's cute. I can't help it."

"Be gone, traitor." Janessa waved her off with a pretense of hurt feelings that quickly lifted into a smile. "Go on. I'm sure Hank's waiting for you."

As Andra headed into the stands, Owen came from the direction of the barn, leading his horse, Casper.

Janessa gave him a warm smile. "This is it. Are you ready?"

He nodded. "I figure even if we don't win, the worst we can do is take second."

She laughed. "That's true." Looking past Owen, she saw Micah and Keely riding into the holding area behind the steer chute. She blinked and looked away. Sensing that Owen had noticed them, too, she forced a bright smile. "Things seem to be going well for you and Keely. I guess the plan worked."

"Yeah. It's been good getting to know her better." He looked down shyly. "But actually, this stopped being about impressing Keely a few weeks ago."

"Really?"

"Yeah. Once I started to get the hang of the roping, I realized I needed to do this for me. You know, to prove to myself that I could do it." His eyes met hers. "Thanks for believing in me. That really means a lot."

Her heart warmed. Even if Micah *had* tricked her into doing this, good things were coming out of it anyway. "You're welcome. Oh, and thanks for helping to fix up my truck."

"It was all Micah's idea." Owen glanced over at Micah, who was riding in small circles just outside the box where Janessa, then he, would start the event. "I wondered why we didn't see you after the parade. Micah told me he thought you were upset about something."

She shrugged. "It's not a big deal." She hoped her face didn't reveal the truth. It was embarrassing that she'd let herself get hurt and this was going to take some time to get over.

The voice on the loudspeaker announced that there would be one more tie-down roper before the team roping. A whoop went up from the crowd and Owen smiled nervously. "Casper and I had better go get into position."

"Okay." She gave him a quick hug. "See you out there."

He started to go, then turned back. "Oh, and Janessa."

"Yeah?"

"Don't be too hard on Micah. I mean, he's a bull rider. He's fallen on his head more than the average guy."

She gave him another encouraging smile. As he headed toward the heeler's box, she put a hand on either side of Molly's muzzle and rested her forehead on the horse's face. "What do you think, girl? Are we ready for this?"

Easing in a breath, she asked for God's strength for all four of them. *Well...*she glanced upward. *Eight if you include the horses.* She paused, looking up again. *Okay, ten if you include the steers. Just help us all to do our best, Lord.* She put her foot in the stirrup and pulled herself into the saddle. She turned to start Molly for the holding area, but tugged the reins as Micah made another circle on his horse and happened to meet her eyes just as Janessa looked at him. She quickly glanced away, then added to her prayer. *And help me to forgive Micah for being a...well, for being the way he is. Amen.*

Urging Molly closer to the holding area where Micah was warming up his horse, she felt his eyes drilling into her. Her stomach clenched.

"Well, hey, Janessa." His voice sounded tentative.

She bit her lip, then wished him luck and kept going. She couldn't risk his saying something that might cloud her thinking, especially not right before her event.

Moving into the safety of the header's box, she released her rope from the strap on her saddle. With cheers and whoops filling her ears, she made a few practice swings. While the announcer talked to the enthusiastic crowd about the history of team roping, Janessa drew a deep breath and took a look out at the stands.

It had always been a habit of hers to look up right before her event to find her family. When she was little, Mama, Daddy and Adam had always been there to cheer her on. For her last ten rodeos, she had counted on Mama and Adam's show of support. Now, as she caught sight of her brother sitting with his arm around Courtney, and

Mama probably explaining the nuances of the rodeo to Mr. Bloom, the melancholy that had been niggling her seemed strangely absent. No one would ever replace her daddy, and Mr. Bloom wasn't trying to. Just like Courtney, he had been doing a great job of carving out his own place in their family. Mama had been a widow for eleven years and she deserved to be happy.

Her eyes burning a little, Janessa clasped her throat, momentarily forgetting that the diamond heart wasn't there. She slid her fingers down the chain and felt the cross, thanking God for His unwavering assurance that she would one day be reunited with her daddy in heaven.

Peace fell over her. It was time to let go and move ahead.

A loud clanking sound jolted her from her thoughts. The first steer had just been moved into the chute, and the solid gate behind it secured.

Adrenaline surged. As the announcer called out her name then Owen's, the audience roared.

She leaned down to talk to Miss Molly. "Let's go, baby. This is it." Taking a few more practice swings, she looked all around the stands, seeing banners hailing support of Our Hometown Team as the boisterous audience took to their feet.

Her breath jammed in her throat. The town hadn't abandoned her after all. Reenergized, she looked over at Owen to make sure he was ready.

Taking in a deep breath, she made eye contact with the gatekeeper who awaited her cue to release the steer. She nodded.

Instantly, the animal bolted from the chute. Miss Molly took off at a full run and Janessa started to swing her rope over her head. With her focus totally fixed on the steer, she threw the loop, making a clean horn catch. In one fluid movement, she wrapped her rope around the saddle horn and turned Miss Molly to the left, forcing the steer into position for Owen.

She held her breath as Owen made his swing. The rope sailed under the steer's back legs, looking as if only one caught, but when they pulled their ropes taut, both legs were in. The crowd went wild, and a look of relief passed over Owen's face. Janessa couldn't have been more proud of him.

There was an audible *shush* from the stands they trotted their horses out of the arena and listened for their score.

"And that will be 7.2 seconds for the team of Greene and West."

A wave of joy passed through her. The best she and Owen had done in practice was seven point five seconds, which had felt lightning fast. She and Owen, who only a few weeks before had possessed zero confidence in his ability, had beaten their best practice time.

As she quickly dismounted and threw her arms around Owen, they both spoke at once.

"We did it, Janessa—"

"Nice roping!"

"And now for the team of Brody and Rogers." The announcer could barely be heard over the hoots and hollers of the spectators.

Janessa and Owen stood with bated breath as both Keely and Micah held their ropes up, and the second steer stood at the ready.

Micah nodded to the gatekeeper, and the chute clanged open. Another round of cheers went up from the stands as the steer ran for all it was worth, kicking up a cloud of dust. In a second, Micah and Keely were off, too, with their ropes swinging over their heads. Caught up in the excitement, Janessa yelled encouragement as Micah expertly made his throw. The loop encircled the animal's horns, and Janessa flung her arms in the air.

In the next instant, Micah dallied and turned the steer to the left, then Keely threw her loop under the hind legs, easily catching them both. Janessa let out another yell, thrilled for Keely's success.

"That's 6.5 seconds for the team of Brody and Rogers, making them the winners of today's team-roping event." The announcement prompted a deafening cheer from the crowd and a beauty queen smile from Keely.

The pair brought their horses in and dismounted amidst an incoming tide of people waving cameras, microphones and autograph books.

Janessa threw an arm around Owen. "I'm sorry we didn't win."

"It's okay." He shrugged. "All that really matters to me is that I didn't fall on my face. Sometimes winning means something other than making the best time."

As soon as she could break away from the minifrenzy that was mainly focused on Micah, Keely darted over to them.

"Congratulations, Keely." Janessa gave her a hug. "You were amazing."

"Thanks. I couldn't have done it without you guys. I feel like we're all a team. Like all four of us won."

Looking over at Micah, who stood at the center of the mass of fans and media people, Janessa had to admit that she felt the same. No matter how things had turned out she'd learned an awful lot from him, and the past five weeks had been a lot of fun.

When she drew her attention away from Micah, Owen was in the middle of rehashing his first rodeo experience with Keely. "That was the low point of my life when I looked up and saw you laughing at me."

"What are you talking about?" Keely's brow furrowed. "I didn't laugh at you. I felt terrible for you."

"But…" Owen's eyes crinkled in confusion. "You had your hand over your mouth."

"So you assumed I was laughing?" She gave his arm a slug. "You big dope. Other people were laughing because they thought it was a trick that you had planned. I knew it was an accident and my hands just flew to my face. I never laughed."

"Oh." Owen still seemed puzzled. "But, why wouldn't you ever talk to me after that?"

"Are you kidding?" Her hands plunked onto her hips. "You never gave me a chance. Every time I'd see you, you'd run the other way or hide behind something."

"Well, I'll be." Owen tipped back his hat and gazed at her. "All these years, I thought you were ignoring me."

"It's a little hard to ignore someone who's making such a big show of avoiding you." Keely's blue eyes sparkled with a hint of flirtation. "Honestly, I always thought that was pretty cute."

Owen looked down and scuffed the toe of his boot in the dirt. "So, you want to go on some carnival rides with me after the award ceremony?"

She smiled and held out her hand. "It's about time you asked."

As they turned to lead their horses back to the barn, Owen flashed Janessa a triumphant smile.

Janessa wanted to burst with happiness for them.

She pivoted to give Molly a pat on the nose, and saw that the crowd around Micah had dwindled down to mostly giddy girls who were rattling on and waving pieces of paper for him to sign. He smiled and chatted with them, clearly in his element.

It crossed her mind that she could just hang out till he

was finished. What harm could it do to let him know that after all was said and done, she was grateful she'd competed and that he'd been right all along about Owen and Keely.

No sooner had she made this decision than Carly, with her hair teased up even bigger than the night before, shouldered her way through the throng of women and threw her arms around Micah.

Janessa's heart sank. The guy had his own life. It was best for her to just steer clear.

After the rodeo and the award ceremony, Janessa spent the rest of the afternoon either going on carnival rides with Andra and Hank, or playing midway games with Adam and Courtney. While she appreciated being included, rolling along like a third wheel had left her feeling pretty flat.

Now as she sat with her family and a group of friends at a long table in the picnic area that had been roped off for the chili feed and barbecue cook-off, the festive atmosphere presented a stark contrast to her mood.

Try as she might to stay focused on the conversations around her, her mind kept wandering. If what Carly had said about Micah returning to the rodeo circuit was true, why hadn't he mentioned it? They'd talked a lot over the past several weeks, and every time the topic of his bull-riding career had come up, he'd always spoken of it in the past tense. But maybe Carly was right. Maybe his time in Thornton Springs had just been a diversion while he finished recovering from his accident.

And maybe Janessa had just been a side note to that diversion.

She shook herself. What did it matter anyway? As soon as she had her details worked out, she would be moving on, too. Whatever Micah Brody chose to do with his life was really none of her concern.

In an attempt to refocus her thoughts, she scanned the crimson-, gold- and purple-streaked sky and envisioned herself in Seattle. But somehow, all she could conjure was a picture of gray skies and endless rain. Sighing, she tuned back in to the conversations at the table.

Andra was lamenting to Hank about her missed opportunity to rent the candy kitchen, since she hadn't found any other suitable place in town. Adam and Courtney debated about which of the several bowls of chili they had in front of them was the tastiest. And Mama was describing her vision for redecorating the Circle-O ranch house to Mr. Bloom, who seemed to be receiving her ideas with enthusiasm.

As Janessa took a bite of chili and tried to navigate this conversational landscape, her phone beeped, announcing a text. She shoved her bowl aside and removed her phone from her purse.

Hana. Her stomach knotted like a kaiser roll. Ever since the "luxury apartment" had fallen through, her future roommate had gotten quirkier with each communication. Bracing herself, Janessa read the message.

I found a 1 bdrm apartment 4 $750 a month!

One bedroom? Maybe she could live with that. She typed back, Gr8.

A moment later, another text came through.

Not the best naybrhood, bt it seems safe enuf.

Seems? She read on.

Jst 1 ctch. We'll hav2 gt a c@.

A cat? She texted back. No prob. I lov c@s. Then she thought about it. Y? R thr mice?

No.

She raised a finger to type Gud, but before she could, another message came through.

Bigr.

Bigger? Bigger than mice? What did this apartment have? Wolverines?

She responded. U mean u found us an apartment that has RATS?

The escalating pitch of Andra's voice shifted Janessa's attention from her screen. "Cynthia and Skylar almost have their new kitchen finished." She shook her head, eliciting an empathetic look from Hank. "Then their old space will finally be ready for the dentist to move in."

Looking down again, Janessa breathed fire at her suddenly silent phone. She needed to know if she should readjust her thinking to accommodate the kind of roomies who didn't pay rent.

"You know what this town needs?" Courtney spoke through a mouthful of chili. "A bakery."

A round of agreement circled the table.

Andra clicked her tongue. "If that *dentist* hadn't come along, someone could have turned the candy kitchen into a great little bakery café. Don't tell Joe, but we could use an alternative to the diner in this town."

Huffing out exasperation, Janessa glanced up to see Courtney hand Adam her chili bowl.

"Get the five-star this time, honey."

"Seriously, Court." Janessa arched a brow at her sister-in-law as she impatiently typed U still there? into her phone. "That's your fourth bowl, and you've gotten it hotter every time. At this rate, we're going to have to call the fire department."

When there was no response, Janessa looked up, catching a meaningful exchange between Courtney and Adam.

Lowering her phone, she narrowed her eyes. "What are you guys up to?"

Adam took in a long breath, then cleared his throat. "Does anyone know the population of Thornton Springs?"

The question completely diverted Janessa's attention from her worries about rodents. "Weird time for a geography lesson, bro."

"*I* know." Owen glanced at Keely like he hoped this would impress her. "Somewhere in the neighborhood of twenty-five hundred."

Adam nodded. "Twenty-six seventeen to be exact."

Mama had stopped talking about lace curtains and was regarding Adam and Courtney with a look of restrained suspicion. "What are you getting at, honey?"

Janessa's phone beeped again, but she set it facedown next to her chili.

A roguish smile crept onto Adam's face as he traded another look with Courtney. "We want you all to be the first to know that sometime in April, the population will be increasing to twenty-six eighteen."

The table fell silent for a moment, then Janessa shrieked. "I'm going to be an aunt!"

All at once, Adam and Courtney were caught up in a whirlwind of congratulations, back slapping and hugs.

Janessa jumped to her feet and ran around the table, throwing herself into what felt like a giant group embrace. She took a step back, allowing the news to settle. This was amazing…and *terrible.* With a hurricane force, the deeper implications of this surprising turn of events hit. Her family was going to go on living, with a new baby and everything, and she'd be a million miles away.

Okay, not quite a million, but it might as well be. She blinked back a smorgasbord of emotions that threatened to overwhelm her. How, in all her planning, had she not anticipated this?

Feeling suddenly wiped out, she stepped toward the group of women encircling Courtney and discussing possible baby shower dates. She tugged at Andra's arm. "I think I'm going to call it a night."

Andra's face fell. "You're not staying for the fireworks?"

She shook her head. "I'm really not in a fireworks kind of mood. Will you tell everyone good-night for me?"

After Andra agreed and returned to the debate over gender-neutral shower themes, Janessa made her way around the table to retrieve her abandoned phone. Numbly, she picked it up and remembered the unread message. She clicked it on and read.

I've changd my mind. I can't liv w sum1 as moody n unpredictable as u.

Her stomach plummeted into her handcrafted black leather roper boots. What on earth did Hana mean by that? She read on.

You'll hav2 fnd sum1 else 2 do yr legwork 4 u, Miss Hard-2-please.

Hard to please? Confusion slapped her like a cold gust of wind. She started to type a response, then stopped. Instead, her eyes turned upward and she mouthed *Thank You.*

She was off the hook. She'd been released from the obligation to live with a person who was clearly not a good match for her. Relief seeped through her veins.

The relief lasted about a second before reality burst through her carefully constructed dam of denial. Now not only did she not have an apartment, but she didn't have a roommate, either. If the best her budget would allow was one half of a rat-infested one-bedroom in a questionable neighborhood, it was clear that she couldn't afford to live by herself. She looked up again. *I'm giving this one to You, Lord.*

On the heels of that thought, she swiveled around and ran smack into a solid pillar of blue plaid cowboy shirt. Looking up into Micah's startlingly cerulean eyes, she froze.

For a moment, he looked as surprised as she felt. Then he took a step back and arched a brow at the ongoing hullabaloo behind her. "What's going on?"

Feeling a heat wave wash her cheeks, she glanced behind him, relieved that there was no sign of Carly.

She forced a guarded smile. "Turns out I'm going to be an aunt."

As they exchanged congratulations, over the new family member for her and the rodeo win for him, Janessa puzzled over what he was doing there. Had he sought her out to finish the conversation she'd cut short last night during the parade? Now that she was calmer she'd at least be able to listen, but that didn't mean she could let her defenses down.

Remembering what Carly had told her, she felt the painfully familiar sting of loss. As much as she had thought she was getting closer to Micah over the past few weeks, she'd been wrong to think she really knew him. Maybe everything was a sport to him—rodeos, relationships, keeping his dad at arm's length.

But if Micah had Carly, and God only knew how many other women, willing to play the game on his terms, why would he even bother with Janessa? And why couldn't she just let go?

She felt like a bull rider, struggling to hang on to the bull rope even after getting bucked off. And the bull was bucking so hard, she couldn't find the ground. The smart thing would be to just let go, but that felt dangerous, too. So there she was just hanging on with her feet, and her heart dragging in the dirt.

With a jolt, she realized that he was eyeing her expectantly. She forced her voice out past a lump that had formed in her throat. "So I guess you won the deal. So much for me getting to drive your truck." She wanted to sound worldly and aloof, but her forced lightheartedness sounded as disingenuous as it felt.

"You know..." He leaned in slightly to be heard over the noise around them. "We never shook on it. I can't really expect you to stay here because of that..."

Disappointment coursed through her. She wanted him to prod her about coming through on her end of the deal even though she'd never actually agreed to it. Suddenly, a part of her wished that she had.

She shrugged. "It wouldn't matter now anyway." Her attempt at sounding nonchalant came out sounding decidedly...well...*chalant.* "I don't need a new car now that I have Old Blue. I mean, what's wrong with driving a vintage truck around?"

The corners of his mouth curved down in contemplation. "Nothing that I can see."

She swallowed so hard it made her throat hurt. She had to make it clear that she considered his fixing her truck to be a job he'd done for her, not a gift. She balled up her fists to keep her hands from shaking. Then they spoke simultaneously.

"You'll have to let me know—"

"I just wanted to tell you—"

"Janessa!"

Startled, she looked past Micah to see Tandy hurrying down the crowded midway, waving something that looked like a sheet of white paper.

Janessa exchanged a look of confusion with Micah, then moved around him to meet Tandy at the entrance to the picnic area.

Mama was at her side in an instant. "What is it, Tandy?"

Catching her breath, Tandy clutched what Janessa could now see was a large envelope. "I went to the Bar-G to feed the dogs and grab the mail. I'm glad I did, because look what was in it."

She presented the envelope to Janessa as people in the immediate area hushed each other and started to crowd around or shift in their seats to get a better view.

Reaching out to take it, Janessa stared at the upper left-hand corner, where a fancy scroll revealed the sender.

Mama put her hands to her cheeks and gasped, then lifted her head to announce, "It's from her school!"

A clatter rose up from the crowd, followed by another round of shushes. Suddenly, everything was quiet except the clanking from the barbecue pit and the distant happy shrieks of people riding the Tilt-A-Whirl or the Ferris wheel. Everyone leaned in, waiting for her to open it.

Her heart beat like a galloping steed as she gaped at the envelope in her hands. This wasn't the skinny kind that delivers college rejections. This was the big fat kind. The kind that contains notices of acceptance.

With shaky hands she pealed back the flap, unable to hold in the tears that had conspired to totally humiliate her in front of a good percentage of the town. She pulled out a stack of crisp white papers, and read from the top one. "'Dear Miss Greene, We are pleased to inform you…'"

The crowd around her broke into whooping and shouting, as the words on the page faded to a gray blur. She'd done it. She'd gotten accepted into Le Cordon Bleu.

As people hugged and congratulated her, she searched the crowd through tear-filled eyes. Micah stood on the outskirts, shifting from one foot to the other and looking down. When his eyes finally met hers, he smiled sadly and turned to leave.

Part of her wanted to run after him and part of her wanted to just let him go. It was impossible at the moment to tell which part had her best interests at heart.

Chapter 11

Micah walked out onto the carnival midway feeling worse than he'd ever felt in his life. For a guy who'd lost his mom as a kid and had been stomped on by a two thousand pound bull that was saying a lot.

Since there really wasn't any reason for him to stick around the fairgrounds now, he started for the parking lot behind the horse barn. Looking up at the big Montana sky that was slipping toward sundown, he reflected on all the things he'd learned about himself since coming to Thornton Springs. Too bad one of the most important lessons had come to him too late.

He'd been all set last night to tell Janessa how wrong he'd been about not wanting a serious relationship. That she'd been right—what he'd said to her about being afraid of losing someone like she'd lost her daddy applied to him, too. That was exactly why he'd been running all this time. He couldn't stand the thought of getting hurt again.

He had wanted to tell her that he was hoping she might feel the same. And that she might reconsider her options.

Then he'd gotten distracted by the arrival of his dad and Carly, which couldn't have come at a worse time. And when Janessa had gotten upset, he had figured he should wait until after the rodeo to talk to her. It was never good to try to talk to someone about anything serious right before they competed—a fact that had come in handy for both him and his dad over the years. Since he'd been perpetually gearing up for the next event in the next town, they had always put off talking about the heavy stuff. The result was a lifetime of issues that had never gotten dealt with. No wonder he had ultimately needed to get untangled from his knotted-up rope of a life.

After the rodeo and the award ceremony, he had kept busy getting the horses back to the ranch, but had gone looking for Janessa tonight. He'd wanted to take one more crack at having that talk with her. Why had he put it off? Now that she knew she'd been accepted into her school, any hope he'd had of her changing her plans was shot.

Not that he wasn't happy for her. He was. She had wanted to go to that school long before he had even met her. Why should he expect her to stay here just for him? No, it was best for him to step back and let her get on with her life.

He approached the barn, shaking his head at life's ironies. In just a few short weeks, he'd helped Owen become confident enough to win the girl of his dreams, and he himself had become what Owen had been when they'd first met. A one-woman kind of guy who'd totally blown it.

As he rounded the corner into the parking lot, he caught sight of a familiar figure leaning against the side of his truck. *Just great.* It was too late to turn around and go back the other way. His dad had already seen him. Hadn't he made it clear last night that he didn't have anything more to say to him?

When he was close enough to speak without having to raise his voice, Micah said, "Where's Carly?"

His dad straightened, as if trying unsuccessfully to claim some height over his son. "She's waiting back in her motel room."

Micah felt his jaw tighten. "Why on earth did you bring her up here with you, anyway?"

"I thought she'd be able to persuade you if you wouldn't listen to me. Besides, she was as worried about you as I was. She's the one who read about you being in this little rodeo. If she hadn't called me, I'd still be trying to find you."

Micah's gaze turned pointed. "Yeah, well did it ever occur to you that maybe I didn't want you to find me?"

"Come on, son." It was clear from his dad's hard demeanor that he had heard Micah's question but was choosing to ignore it. "Carly's waiting for us to pick her up so we can get on the road."

Weary from their exchange the night before, not to mention the ebbing adrenaline from the rodeo, Micah leaned an arm on the hood of his truck. "Dad, I told you last night. I'm not going back with you."

His dad shook his head. "Oh come on, son. You've made your point. It's time to come back to reality. People are counting on you. You still have a shot at the nationals, but you can't afford to waste any more time."

Micah shook his head. "It's not a waste, Dad."

A shadow went across his dad's face, reminding Micah of the way he looked when he was up against an animal that was too strong-willed to be tamed. "So you're willing to just throw away everything we worked for all these years?"

Anger painted a dismal coat of gray over Micah's resolve. "Don't you even want to know why I left?"

He gave a passive one-shoulder shrug. "You got scared. It happens. But it's only going to get worse the more time you let pass. You leave with me tonight, you can be back in shape to compete in a few weeks."

Micah's chest squeezed. Why was his dad making this so difficult? He looked him square in the eye. "Do you even care about what I want?"

"You don't know what you want. You're not thinking straight."

Heaving out a breath, Micah stepped forward to unlock his door. "I'm not arguing with you, Dad."

"You know, you could have at least told me you were leaving." His dad swept his hand down the length of the Dodge. "When I realized your truck was gone from the house, I assumed someone had stolen it. I went to that place where you were staying—"

"It was the rehabilitation center, Dad. You make it sound like I was at the Hilton."

He sighed, making a show of how patient he was being. "I went to tell you that your truck was missing. Imagine my surprise when they said you weren't there."

"Yeah, Dad. I can imagine." The hoped-for impact of his sudden disappearance had been part of the point.

"So I started talking to people. No one seemed to know anything except Carly."

He closed his eyes and rubbed his jaw. Carly had promised him she wouldn't say anything, but maybe that had been asking too much of her.

"It was bad enough you being out all those weeks. But the doctors were just about ready to okay you getting back in the ring. Now you set yourself that much more behind. Meanwhile, other guys have been winning. The longer you're gone, the more you feed their confidence."

"All right, all right." Micah slammed his hand down on the hood of his truck. "I'm sick of you treating me like I'm only as good as my last score."

"You're a bull rider." His dad's eyes smoldered holes into him. "You *are* only as good as your last score."

Micah willed his heart to translate his feelings into words that his dad would understand. "I'm more than just a bull rider, Dad. I'm your *son*."

The look in his dad's eyes burned hot then smoldered, like a campfire that had been doused with water. The silence stretched as he seemed to let Micah's words sink in. When he spoke again, the intensity of his voice had tapered off some. "You know, I've done the best I could."

A shiver of disquiet ran through Micah as he studied his dad. He was so used to the man's cold emotional detachment that he found the slight edge of pain in his voice alarming.

His dad rubbed a hand across one side of his face then the other. "Ever since your mom died..." He trailed off and held for a stretch, as if to pull up some long-buried memory. "You've been all I have."

Micah's stomach tensed. This was the first time he could actually remember his dad showing any real emotion. Remorse gushed through him at the lengths he'd had to go to in order to awaken it. "I never meant to hurt you, Dad."

Still gazing off in the distance, his dad gave a slow nod. "I just wanted to make a life for you."

Micah's mind went ahead of his words, testing for potential emotional land mines. "We could have stayed on the ranch, you know. That was a life."

The suggestion was met with a slow shake of the head. "There was nothing left for us there, boy. Not after she was gone."

Stiffening, Micah's mind stumbled down the various paths this conversation could take. He settled on the one that felt the most compassionate, a sentiment he hadn't known he possessed toward this man. "It's okay to miss her, Dad. I miss her, too." When that was received with a silent nod, he continued. "It's just that I tried so hard to please you, but it was never good enough."

That snapped his dad to attention. "Never good enough? You're a champion."

"I know that." A wave of unhealed pain surged up in him and mingled with the guilt that had shadowed him since he'd left Texas. "But I want to be good enough even when I don't win. I want you to be proud of me because I'm your son. Not because I managed to make more points than anyone else."

His dad stared, with the barest hint of moisture rimming his eyes. "I've always been proud of you. I thought you knew that."

The words stretched across Micah's mind, their meaning slowly taking hold. His dad had *always* been proud of him. Emotion filled his throat, threatening to crowd out his response even as it formed. "You never said it. You were always pushing me. Always telling me I should be doing better."

"I only pushed you because I thought that was what you needed. It takes a tough mind to make it as a bull rider. You can't afford to let any negative thoughts in."

"I'm sure you're right, Dad. You taught me a lot about not giving up." Micah felt the walls of defensiveness he'd spent years reinforcing crack like clay under the hot sun. "I just think it's time to apply that to other areas of my life." He paused, weighing how much he wanted to divulge. "I feel called to do some things that could make a real difference."

"Huh." His dad frowned, letting that thought settle.

"Besides," he went on. "It's not like you need me. You've gotten yourself pretty well established with the stock contractors."

His dad nodded, apparently pleased that the conversation had turned to more stable ground. "The right stock is important. People don't realize it takes a skill to transport those animals."

"You're real good at it, too. I've always been impressed with the way you managed to support us all those years."

A smile curved his dad's lips. "I just never thought I'd see the day you'd willingly give up bull riding."

"I'm a little surprised, too, but I'm getting used to the idea."

His dad gave him a cat-eyed look. "This wouldn't have anything to do with that young lady you were with last night, would it?"

Micah's breath caught in the space between his lungs and his throat, intensifying a dull pain that had been sitting there for the past half hour. "I wish I could say yes, but it looks like that's not going to work out."

"I'm sorry to hear that. Because I'll tell you the truth…" He placed a strong, affirming hand on Micah's shoulder. "As much as it hurt to lose your mother, I wouldn't trade my memories of her for anything. When you find the right person, that's God's greatest blessing."

Micah furrowed his brow. "You mean that? I always thought you blamed God for taking her away from us."

His dad nodded. "It's taken a while, but I'm finally starting to think I might have been wrong about that. I might be a stubborn old coot, but I'm not completely hopeless."

"I'm glad to hear that. You know, Mom would be really pleased if you'd show your face in a church every once in a while."

His expression warmed. "I might just do that."

As the nice moment resolved into a comfortable silence, something sparked in Micah's heart. "Dad." His voice was slow. Contemplative. "Do you have another minute? There's something I'd like to run by you."

His dad's look turned pensive, then pleased. "For you, son, I've got all the time in the world."

As Janessa's crowd of well-wishers started to dissipate, a panic crept up on her. What if Micah was leaving tonight? What if that was what he'd come to tell her and she hadn't given him a chance?

Telling everyone she was exhausted, which was true, she headed out of the picnic area and down the midway. She'd seen Micah's truck in the parking lot behind the barn when she parked there herself earlier in the day. If it was still there she would know he hadn't left the fairgrounds.

As twilight ticked toward darkness, she shouldered her way through the carnival crowd. Why did she feel such a desperate need to see him? She wanted to move on, to make a clean break. Didn't she?

Her truck. That was it. She couldn't let him leave town without making an arrangement to pay for the work he'd done on Old Blue. Her mouth tightened as she tried to convince herself that was all she needed to say.

She rounded the corner of the barn and stopped. There stood Micah next to his Dodge, engaged in what looked like a serious conversation with his dad. She scooted back, leaning forward just enough to keep the men in her scope.

Straining to make out the words that were flying back and forth between them, she took a quick glance around the lot. No sign of Carly. *Thank goodness.*

And no chance of making out what the men were discussing, either. That was just as well, since eavesdropping was probably some sort of sin. It didn't look like they were arguing, like the night before. In fact, their body language seemed to indicate that things were downright amiable between them. She thought she even heard a laugh rise up on the evening air.

After a moment, the two men shook hands, as if they'd just completed a business transaction. Then Mr. Brody got into another truck that was just as nice as Micah's but slightly more road worn. Micah stood there for a moment, looking caught up in his thoughts.

Before she could lose her courage, she darted out from the shadows. Even in the faint light from the streetlamps which dotted the small lot, she could see that his eyes lit up when he saw her.

Clasping her elbows, she nodded in the direction his dad had gone. "That looked encouraging."

"It was." A smile lifted. "I think we're on the way to mending some fences."

Her heart warmed at the news. "That's really great." For an instant, things were the way they'd been before, when they'd enjoyed an ease together that had made her feel as if they'd known each other for far longer than a few short weeks.

As quickly as that feeling came it was lost, as she recalled her realization that she'd been nothing particularly special to him.

She cleared her throat. "So, I just wanted to talk to you about..."

He waited, watching her with a keen interest.

With great effort, she forced the quiver from her voice. "You'll have to let me know how to reach you, so I can send you payments." She finished, out of breath and feeling awkward.

"Payments?" His brow furrowed. "For what?"

She tried not to dwell on how cute that made him look. "For my truck."

"Oh." He gave a long blink of understanding. "I told you, I don't expect anything for that."

Carly's message from last night hung in her ears like an annoying hum after an explosion. *I've been there for him through so many long nights.* How was she supposed to get past that?

Her eyelids gritted. "I just don't feel right about it. I mean, it's not like you're my..." She clamped the gate shut on the word she'd been about to say. Not my *boyfriend* or anything. Yeah, that would have scared him right onto the next stagecoach out of Dodge.

He slanted her a questioning look. "Not your *what?*"

She pulled back her shoulders, determined not to get sucked into the quagmire of his rodeo-boy appeal again. "Not my *brother*...or anything."

He nodded, as a point ticked on the *Janessa* side of the invisible scoreboard. Taking in a deep breath, his face turned serious. "Look, Janessa. I had the idea of fixing up your truck for you because you're...you know."

She waited. Because she was what? In need of reliable transportation? That was apparent. But what else was he driving at? "Because I'm *what?*"

He rubbed the back of his neck, obviously not used to women who made him delve any deeper into his vocabulary than *"Well, hey."*

He shrugged. "Because you're...special."

Special? Her eyes narrowed. Did he mean "my-one-and-only" special, or "my-gal-in-Montana" special? As long as there was a question, she had to assume the latter.

Folding her arms, she heaved a sigh. "So, when are you leaving?"

"Leaving?"

"Heading back to the rodeo."

Confusion creased his forehead. "Why would you assume that?"

Resentment brewed. She hated feeling like a pawn in his game. "Because, of Carly. I mean, she's pretty 'special,' too, right?"

He started to speak, then stopped. An array of emotions splashed across his face, ending with amusement, which seemed to be the one to stick. "Janessa. It's not what you're thinking."

"Oh really?" She looked at him. "What am I thinking?" Suddenly gifted with a surge of boldness, she forged ahead. "That you see a lot of girls and that you always make sure they know you don't want anything serious? You need to make that message a little clearer, because I don't think Miss Texas got the memo."

"Janessa, it's not that way, really."

"Oh, no? Well, let me tell you something about women. Any woman who's there for a man through 'lots of long nights when he can't sleep and needs to talk—'" she made air quotes around that part for effect "—is going to be expecting that man to think of her as 'special.' If he doesn't, then he's what women like me consider to be a real jerk."

He stood there, scrunching up his eyes and apparently hitting the replay button on what she'd just said. "So…you think that *Carly*—"

"Carly told me herself, so don't try to lie to me."

The crinkles fell away from his face and he let out a laugh.

"You think that's funny?"

"No. Janessa—"

"Well, is it true or not?"

"Yeah, it's true, but—"

"Okay, then."

"It's true that she was there for me through lots of long nights when I couldn't sleep." He paused, dipping down to force eye contact. "I couldn't sleep because I was in so much pain after my accident."

Her stomach clenched like a fist as she turned for her car. She really didn't need to hear this.

"Janessa, listen." He grabbed her arm, forcing her to stop and face him. "Carly was the night nurse at the rehab center where I went to recover. Yeah, she listened to me talk because that was her job."

She stopped, allowing the impact of what he'd just said to soak in. She wanted to say something to reverse her downward spiral into utter humiliation, but all that came out was, "Oh."

"And I'm not going back to the rodeo." His voice was soft and reassuring.

"You're not?"

He shook his head. "Nope."

"But…" Her mind raced as she tried to call up all her reasons for being mad at him. "Carly said she was going to be handling your PR."

He rolled his eyes skyward. "Apparently, my dad told her that if she could talk me into going back to Texas, he'd put her on the payroll. I never agreed to that, and I told her last night she needs to go back to her nursing job. She's good at it. And if you're wondering if there was any hope of a romance between her and me…"

She bit her lower lip.

"It was strictly one-sided. I've actually been the Lone Ranger for quite some time."

"Oh." That thought settled nicely. She looked up. "So… if you're not going back to the rodeo…"

"I got an idea a few weeks back and it's just stuck in my head. I can't shake it. Then tonight…" He waved an arm in the direction of where his dad's truck had been parked. "I got some real affirmation that this is the right way to go."

"What is it?"

"Well, I've been thinking about buying a little ranch and starting up some kind of program for kids to learn about animals. Maybe even teach them some rodeo skills."

"You're starting a junior bull-riding school?"

He laughed. "No bulls. Maybe a sheep or two. I thought I'd offer some sort of scholarship for the kids who can't afford it. You know, as my way of giving back."

It warmed her to think of how great he was with kids. This was not the same Micah she'd met in her barn earlier in the summer. "Oh. Wow, Micah. That's really great."

He nodded. "The timing is right. I lost my passion for bull riding, and without that, I wouldn't stand a chance of winning."

He met and held her gaze with a sincerity that didn't seem possible to counterfeit. There was something below the surface that not even a veteran Don Juan could pull off believably.

Tears welled in her eyes and a rush of emotion filled her. She realized in that moment, looking into his soul, that she couldn't deny the truth anymore. She had fallen in love with Micah Brody.

This was terrible. It went completely against her plans.

He seemed to get lost in the moment, too, then looked away as if reboarding his train of thought. "And then tonight… when I was talking to my dad, another inspiration struck."

She couldn't speak for fear of bursting into tears, so she just gave him a *go on* look.

"He's worked for other guys for years helping with the rodeo animals. I've just had this feeling that what he really wants is to go into business for himself. So, I asked him if he'd like to go in with me on a ranch. We could work together raising rodeo stock and teaching the kids."

Warmth rushed through her. This seemed so perfect. "And he said yes?"

"He said he loves the idea. We need to talk more about the details, but it sounds like it might just work out."

A potentially immobilizing warmth crept up her spine, and she tore her gaze from his. She had to get away from him before his magnetic pull made leaving impossible. Whether she had misjudged him or not, she had plans. She had to stay the course.

She took a step back, putting herself at a slightly safer distance from him. "I should go. Are you heading home?"

Studying her, he gave a slow shake of his head. "I was, but I'm going to stick around. I have a lot to think about." His eyes warmed in a way that made her stomach jump. "I hear they set off fireworks as soon as it's completely dark." He glanced up at the deep blue blanket that was slowly working its way across the sky toward the pillow of western mountains. "That should be any minute now. I think I'll just head on over to the arena." Giving a half turn of his body, his eyes pooled with an implied invitation.

An alarm went off between her ears, telling her to run while she had the chance. If she stayed, her heart would get lassoed, throwing her life plans for a loop.

She forced a wan smile. "Good night, then." One foot moved in the direction of her car.

He hesitated just enough to make her think he was

going to protest, then touched the brim of his hat and ambled away.

She watched after him for a few seconds, her heart feeling heavy. Just as she started for her car, Andra hurried around the corner of the barn. Seeing Janessa, her shoulders relaxed and she rushed toward her.

"Janessa!" Andra moved with an urgent canter. "I'm glad you're still here."

Janessa took a step toward her, not feeling up to matching her enthusiasm.

"Guess what?" She bounced on her toes. "The dentist is moving to Anaconda."

Janessa frowned, then lowered her voice like they were in a spy movie. "And the fish flies at midnight." She straightened. "What dentist?"

"You know. The one who wanted to rent the candy space. He's moving to Anaconda instead."

"Oh." She forced herself to switch gears with only a modicum of success. "But…isn't the space still too much for your catering business?"

Andra closed her eyes, seeming to mentally retrace her steps so she could catch Janessa up. "Courtney was telling us that her friend Sheila is going to come out for the birth of her baby. You remember Sheila?"

"Of course. Her maid of honor."

"Right. And while she was talking, I remembered what Sheila does for a living."

Slowly, Janessa became fully engaged in the conversation. "She works for a big restaurant design firm in L.A."

"So then it hit me. I asked Courtney to give me Sheila's number, and I called her right then and there. She said she thought it was a brilliant idea and that she'd be happy to help."

Janessa shook her head, still missing a key piece to this puzzle. "Help with what?"

A broad grin crossed Andra's face. "How does this sound—" She spread her hands in front of her face with a directorial flourish. "Golden Pear Café and Catering."

Suddenly, all the pieces fell into place. This was so obvious, yet they had totally missed it. "Andra, that's brilliant."

"Isn't it great?" Andra grabbed her by the elbows and they jumped up and down the way they had when they were kids at a winning soccer game.

"This is so exciting." Slightly out of breath, Janessa stopped bouncing. She looked at her friend. "I knew you'd make your dream come true. I've always admired your determination."

"Really? Because all those times when I felt like giving up, you were the one who kept me going."

Janessa gave her a warm smile. "What are best friends for?"

A sheepish look crept over Andra's face. "I might as well tell you...I'm a little disappointed that you got accepted to your school."

"What?"

"Don't get me wrong." She held up her palms. "I'm excited for you and everything. It's just that I've been secretly hoping for a long time that you'd decide to stay here and go into business with me instead."

Janessa missed whatever Andra said next, as that last bit looped in her head. *Go into business with me.* Why hadn't that ever occurred to her?

Suddenly, the fog in her brain cleared to reveal the picture that had been hidden there all along. Hidden behind her careful, self-seeking plans.

Andra was still talking. "...need to find really good people. Maybe before you go, you can help me interview."

Still sorting out her thoughts, Janessa tossed out a response. "You're right. It's really important that we find just the right crew..."

"Janessa..." Andra leaned over to catch her eye. "Did you just say *we?*"

"We. You. Whatever." Suddenly fully alert, Janessa did an abrupt one-eighty and called back over her shoulder as she quickstepped toward the arena. "I'll be right back!"

"Hey," Andra called out. "Where are you going?"

Without stopping her forward momentum, she spun around to explain. "I have a certain cowboy I need to set straight!"

Breaking into a near run, she dashed around the barn, dodging a couple of kids who were working their way over to the arena. From what she could see of the stands ahead of her, they were pretty much packed full. How on earth did she expect to find Micah?

She had to talk to him tonight. This couldn't wait.

Her eyes darted around the area behind the stands, landing on the lone figure of a cowboy leaning against the fence where she had stood earlier in the day watching the tie-down roping.

She pulled in a breath and yelled. "Micah!"

Straightening, he turned first his head, then his body. A slow smile crept across his face as she galloped toward him, skidding to a stop just short of pinning him up against the fence.

He let out a laugh. "What are you doing?"

Her heart thumped so loud, she was certain he could hear it. "I have to ask you a question." Breathing in shallow spurts, she took a moment to find her voice. "You said you were going to buy a little ranch."

His brows rose to a knot in the middle of his forehead. "Yeah."

"Where? Where are you going to buy this ranch?"

"I thought right around here." The barest hint of a smile found his lips. "Why?"

A laugh spurted out before she could stop it. So much for self-control. "You know—" she cleared her throat "—I got accepted into other schools, not just Le Cordon."

Resting one hand on the fence, his eyes brightened. "Oh, yeah?"

She nodded. "One of them happens to be the community college in Helena. They have a fine culinary program."

He angled his head. "Good to know."

"Yes. And it's only twenty minutes from the Bar-G."

He cautioned a step toward her. "What are you getting at, cowgirl?"

Her hands reached up of their own volition, touching the front of his cowboy shirt as she closed the chasm between them. "That your days of 'nothing serious' are over."

He took her by the shoulders and gazed into her eyes, a corner of his mouth lifting in agreement. Before she knew what was happening, his lips met hers in a kiss that could only be meant to seal a promise.

An earsplitting boom jarred them apart and they looked up to see sparks of vibrant color shooting across the big sky overhead.

They looked at each other and laughed.

He turned mock stern. "Hey, I thought you said if you stayed in this town your life would go nowhere."

"Right." She smiled up at him. "*Nowhere* is exactly where I want to go."

He flashed that dimple of his, and kissed her again.

When they pulled away from the kiss, they wrapped their arms around each other and stood there gazing up at the fireworks. She knew then with absolute certainty that what she'd really wanted all along wasn't to live in Seattle or to go to a fancy school, but to be a chef. She could do that right here at home.

Home—in Thornton Springs.

Chapter 12

Janessa stood in front of the oven holding her cow-mitted hands over her eyes. “I’m afraid to look.”

“You have to face your fear.” Micah’s voice was soft but stern. “Or they’re going to burn.”

She slid the mitts away from her face and glanced at Micah, who had his hand on the oven door handle like a gatekeeper awaiting the signal to open the steer chute. Bracing herself with her cows held up in front of her, she nodded. He opened the oven.

She gasped, then blurted out a laugh. She reached in and pulled out a tray of perfectly puffed *choux* pastries. “We did it!”

“We?” He shut the door and followed her to the butcher block table in the center of the kitchen. “All I did was cheer you on. You’re the one who did it.”

“Then I must have needed the cheering.” She set the pan down on the cooling rack and wiped away a threatening tear with her mitt. "I can't believe it. I finally managed to conquer the cream puff. This is the best Christmas Eve ever."

"I'd have to agree." Rubbing his hands together, he smiled. "So, what do we do now?"

"We let them cool so we can fill them." She set her mitts down next to the pastries and picked up a platter of spinach tortilla sandwich rounds that she'd arranged into the shape of a Christmas tree. She assessed the platter of jalapeño pepper halves filled with barbecued beef and wrapped in bacon, on the table in front of Micah. "Looks good. What do you call them?"

He pondered. "How about Cowboy Canapés?"

"I like it." A smile lifted. "Well, come on, cowboy. We have people to feed."

She led the way from the kitchen into the dining room, where the sliding double doors opened up into the parlor. The two rooms and the foyer beyond brimmed with people—family and guests of the Greene's annual Christmas Eve open house.

She crossed to the large dining table and set her tray down amidst the plates and platters that were already there. Stepping back, she evaluated the delectable display of everything from Tandy's prime rib to Mama's chocolate peppermint cream tartlets.

As she took one of the jalapeño halves from the tray Micah still held, she gave him a good-natured elbow to his ribs. "You know, if you're really nice to me, I might let you feature these at the café."

"I don't know if they're ready for the big time yet." Looking around the room, he lifted the tray and held it out as people approached the table. "What do you think, Dad?"

Looking intrigued, Mr. Brody took one of the hors d'oeuvres and popped it into his mouth. He gazed off contemplatively as he chewed. “Mmm. Good, but something’s missing.”

Andra reached around Micah’s arm and took one. All eyes were on her as she bit into it.

“Ranch dressing,” she proclaimed. “It would cool the jalapeño and add a nice zesty flavor.”

Micah looked impressed. “Ranch dressing. Really.”

Andra nodded. “I have a recipe I can share with you.”

Janessa cleared a space on the table for him to set the tray. “You’re turning into a regular sous chef, Micah. We might be asking you to put in some hours in the kitchen soon.”

He set down the tray and wrapped his arm around her. “It’s not enough that I’m your best customer?”

“Best customer?” Andra grabbed a sandwich roll. “I’d say that’s a toss-up between you and Hank.”

“Come on.” Janessa urged Micah toward the parlor. “Let’s go mingle.”

Just as they crossed the threshold, Owen and Keely entered from the foyer, rubbing their arms to warm up from being outside. Keely shook out her blond hair, which looked damp from the falling snow. They headed toward where Janessa and Micah stood next to the fireplace.

“Hey, Janessa, I have some news.” Owen beamed. “It looks like you’re not the only one who’s going to be going to school in Helena after Christmas.”

“You got into vet school?” Janessa threw her arms around him. “Owen, that’s great!”

Keely gave him a sideways look as she warmed her hands in front of the crackling fire. “It’ll keep him out of trouble while I’m off competing.”

Janessa put an arm around Keely, who had become a good friend over the past several months. Now that Janessa was a part-time student and full-time co-owner of the café,

Keely had taken over most of her teaching. Janessa was grateful, but just a little jealous now that Micah and his dad had finished the heated indoor arena at their ranch. It was perfect for horseback riding and roping practice during the cold winter months.

Adam came in from the dining room just then, carrying a heaping plate of food that he handed to Courtney, who sat on the settee next to Mama.

She smiled at Adam, then looked up at the amused faces around her. "Oh, come on. You know what they say about 'eating for two.'"

"Sweetheart," Mama patted Courtney's knee. "Can you believe that next Christmas, we'll have a toddler in the house? I'm so excited, I can hardly stand it."

Mr. Bloom, who sat next to Mama enjoying a cup of Tandy's nonalcoholic but decadently rich eggnog, gave both women a warm smile. Janessa couldn't help but wonder if the little one would be calling him Grandpa someday. The thought made her smile.

Micah spoke softly in her ear. "Shouldn't we be getting back to the kitchen for the...you know...*surprise?*"

She smiled at him, appreciating the acknowledgment of how much her cream puff success meant to her. She was going to love presenting them for everyone to see.

Arm in arm, they returned to the kitchen.

He went to the sink to wash his hands. "Okay, what do you want me to do?"

"All you have to do is cut them in half, like this—" She grabbed a knife and demonstrated by slicing the top off one of the puffs.

He proceeded to do his part while she crossed to the fridge and took out some whipping cream.

She moved to the counter. "Did I tell you I got a Christmas card from Hana?"

He chuckled. "Is she still living in her mom's basement?"

"No." Shooting him a warning look, she took a mint-green Pyrex bowl out of the cupboard. "As a matter of fact, she got a job at a coffee place in Seattle and moved into that studio apartment she found. I think living alone really suits her."

"Great. That reminds me—" he sliced the top off another puff and eyed it critically "—I got a card from Carly."

"Oh?" Pouring the cream into the bowl, Janessa tried to keep the slight hint of jealously out of her voice. She could tell by the raised-brow look he gave her that she hadn't been entirely successful. "I didn't know she had your new address." She took out the hand mixer and plunked the beaters into the cream. Flicking the switch up to High, she unintentionally gave Micah a moment to craft his response. The second the cream was fluffy, she shut off the mixer.

"She didn't." Finishing up with the pastries, he picked up a towel and wiped his hands. "She sent it to general delivery."

"Oh." Feigning indifference, she opened the cupboard and took out the confectioners' sugar and vanilla. She added the last two ingredients to the cream, then carried the bowl to the table. As soon as it was stirred, Micah dipped a finger in the bowl.

She swatted at him with her spoon handle. "You want to help?"

"No, I'll just watch you."

She picked up the first puff and removed the top, then filled it with a dollop of whipped cream and replaced the lid.

"We're invited, by the way," he said.

"To what?" Carefully, she centered the first puff on

the special Santa-in-his-sleigh tray she'd selected for her special dessert.

"To the wedding."

She froze, puzzled. "Wedding? Whose wedding?"

"Carly's." He snuck another finger full of cream. "Didn't I tell you? She met a doctor at her rehab center. They're getting married."

Suppressing the urge to yell *Yay!*, Janessa stuck with a sincere, "Oh, that's great." She took the top off another puff and was about to plop some cream into the center of it when something snared her eye and she stopped cold. Dropping the spoon, she drew her hand to her mouth and let out a gasp.

The next thing she knew, Micah had moved around the table and was standing by her side. He reached into the pastry and removed the diamond ring that had been propped up inside it.

Taking hold of the hand she didn't have covering her mouth, he spoke softly. "It sounds like a good idea, don't you think?"

If she could have found her voice, she would have screamed. She was aware of him getting down on one knee, but she couldn't take her eyes off the very familiar jewel in the center of the ring.

"Janessa..." His voice was a gentle refrain outside the blare of her own thoughts. "Will you be my wife?"

Her eyes drifted to his face as the reality of his question washed over her. Fighting back a torrent of tears, she nodded, still unable to speak.

With a smile of relief, he stood and slipped the ring on her finger, then took her face in his hands and kissed her. When their lips parted, she looked down at the ring on her hand, which had at its center a beautiful heart-shaped jewel surrounded by tiny diamonds. "Micah..."

She could barely get his name out through a lump in her throat. "That's my diamond."

He nodded.

"But, where… How did you…" Her mind was swimming. She didn't even know what question to ask first.

"I found it on the sidewalk the night of the parade."

"You did?" She looked into his deep blue eyes. "You mean you've had it all this time?"

He nodded again. "I was going to give it back to you right away, but there wasn't a good time, and then you never mentioned it. I didn't think about it again until I had this idea. You don't mind, do you?"

"No. It's amazing." Tears of joy welled up and spilled down her cheeks. "It's the best thing anybody's ever done for me."

He kissed her forehead. "That's what you said about Old Blue."

She laughed. "Well, cowboy. I guess you've outdone yourself."

Wrapping her arms around him, she held her ring in front of her face and counted her blessings. It was true that she would always have her daddy in her heart, but that didn't mean there wasn't room for Micah. When she met him, he'd been kind of a big shot, dead set on staying a bachelor, but that really didn't matter now. She loved him for the new man he'd become.

And she would love every minute of being Mrs. Big Sky Big Shot.

* * * * *